"You're bleeding. Come with me."

She glanced down, saw a trail of blood down her right leg. "I'll be fine."

"*Ja*, you will," he said, "after I put a bandage on it."

"I don't need your help."

His eyes narrowed and he looked annoyed. He heaved a sigh. "Would you like me to pick you up and throw you over my shoulder?" he murmured for her ears alone.

"You wouldn't dare!"

"Wouldn't I?"

Face flushing, Charlie glanced around and saw that no one found it odd that she and Nate were having a conversation. The last thing she wanted to do was to cause a scene. She'd done enough impulsive things in her life that had given her parents undue worry. "Fine. Let's not make a big thing of it," she muttered, meeting his gaze.

To her relief, he simply nodded. He didn't look smug that he'd won their argument. In fact, she felt an odd little flutter in her chest when she saw the way he continued to eye her with concern.

Rebecca Kertz was first introduced to the Amish when her husband took a job with an Amish construction crew. She enjoyed watching the Amish foreman's children at play and swapping recipes with his wife. Rebecca resides in Delaware with her husband and dog. She has a strong faith in God and feels blessed to have family nearby. Besides writing, she enjoys reading, doing crafts and visiting Lancaster County.

Books by Rebecca Kertz

Love Inspired

Women of Lancaster County

A Secret Amish Love
Her Amish Christmas Sweetheart
Her Forgiving Amish Heart
Her Amish Christmas Gift

Lancaster County Weddings

Noah's Sweetheart
Jedidiah's Bride
A Wife for Jacob
Elijah and the Widow
Loving Isaac

Lancaster Courtships

The Amish Mother

Her Amish
Christmas Gift

Rebecca Kertz

HARLEQUIN® LOVE INSPIRED®

Recycling programs
for this product may
not exist in your area.

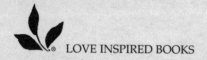 LOVE INSPIRED BOOKS

ISBN-13: 978-1-335-42847-9

Her Amish Christmas Gift

www.Harlequin.com

Printed in U.S.A.

If ye abide in me, and my words abide in you,
ye shall ask what ye will,
and it shall be done unto you.
—*John* 15:7

For my family...those I've known forever
and those I've been happy to meet recently.

And for my ancestors—
without you, I wouldn't be here.

Chapter One

Charlotte Stoltzfus stood near home plate in the makeshift baseball diamond on Abram Peachy's back lawn with the bat inches away from her right shoulder.

"Come on, Charlie!" Joseph shouted. "You can do this, cousin. Keep your eye on the ball and bring Jed and me home."

Meeting his eyes across the distance, she gave a jerk of her head. She wiggled into her stance. And focused. She breathed deeply as she stared at the pitcher, her cousin Noah, and watched him swing back his arm to let the ball fly.

"Aren't you tired of playing with boys?" a male voice said behind her just as she swung her bat.

She growled as she missed. Heart beating wildly, she turned to glare at the man who'd spoken. "Nathaniel Peachy, mind your own business and stop trying to distract me." She was furious. Determined to ignore the one man who got her back up more than anyone on this earth, Charlie breathed to calm herself and got ready for the next pitch.

"Why would I distract you?" Nate said as she swung the bat. She swung and missed again, then she gasped and glared at him.

"Go away," she snapped.

The way he arched an eyebrow made her bristle. She stiffened and became more determined not to let him rattle her. She'd hit the ball despite his presence.

"It's *oll recht*," Jedidiah called out to her. Her eldest cousin, he stood on third base and gazed at her with a smile of reassurance. "Keep your eye on the ball. You can do this."

I can do this. She was a decent player. Isn't that why they first asked her to join the game? *Ignore Nate Peachy. Ignore him. Ignore him.*

Noah watched for her cue. Charlie gave a little nod, and her cousin pitched the ball. She kept it in her sights and swung. The impact made a loud *crack* as wood met leather and sent it sailing over the head of her cousin Daniel near third base, past the stand of trees beyond the property. With a whoop of joy, Joseph ran from second to third as Jedidiah sprinted home. Charlie ran to first base and made it to second then to third, as Nate's younger brother Jacob came out of the bushes with ball in hand. She took a chance, followed Joseph and raced toward home. As the ball headed in her direction, she slid into home plate and grimaced as she felt the sting of a scraped knee.

"Are you *oll recht*?" a deep voice said. She glanced up and saw concern flicker in Nate Peachy's blue eyes. She started to get up and the man was there helping her. "Charlie," he murmured into her ear. "Are you hurt?"

She shook her head, not wanting him to know how much her knee stung and her hip ached from the jolt against the ground.

"Great job, Charlie!" Jed hollered. She grinned at her teammates, who carried on as if she'd won the lottery. Then she looked over at Nate smugly.

"Yahoo!" Joseph yelled. "We won! You never let us down, cousin!"

She forced herself to grin at them with triumph.

Jacob Peachy grumbled good-naturedly as he threw the ball to Noah, who then grabbed the bat and markers they'd used for bases. Jacob met her gaze. "How did you learn to hit a ball like that?"

She shrugged. "From playing with my cousins." She'd been playing baseball with them for over a year. She could still recall the day Joseph had asked her to play and the thrill of her teammates' pleasure when she scored a run.

Jacob shook his head as he smiled. "I should have picked you for my team."

"Now you'll know better for next time." She paused. "If you get the chance," she added. He laughed, then headed to join his friends.

"Charlie." Nate came up from behind her and stood close, too close. "You're bleeding. Come with me."

She glanced down, saw a trail of blood down her right leg. "I'll be fine."

"*Ja*, you will," he said, "after I put a bandage on it."

"I don't need your help."

His eyes narrowed and he looked annoyed. He heaved a sigh. "Would you like me to pick you up and throw you over my shoulder?" he murmured for her ears alone.

"You wouldn't dare!"

"Wouldn't I?"

Face flushing, Charlie glanced around and saw that no one found it odd that she and Nate were having a conversation. The last thing she wanted to do was to cause a scene. She'd done enough impulsive things in her life that had given her parents undue worry. "Fine. Let's not make a big thing of it," she muttered, meeting his gaze.

To her relief, he simply nodded. He didn't look smug that he'd won their argument. In fact, she felt an odd little flutter in her chest when she saw the way he continued to eye her with concern. She followed him at a distance, not wanting to draw attention to the fact that he was leading her into the house. She glanced around and saw the rest of his family outside. She could catch the deacon's wife's attention, have her give her first aid, but she had a feeling that Nate would cause trouble for her if she did. Besides, what was one little bandage, right?

Nate went to the side door and held it open for her. Charlie drew a sharp breath. The man was good-looking; she'd give him that. But those gorgeous blue eyes in a face with fine features under a crop of dark hair weren't what made the man, and she wasn't sure she liked Nate in any way, shape or form. But she'd seen his compassion and tenderness when dealing with his younger sisters. She'd seen it whenever someone needed his help and he'd been right there to assist. And now, to her shock, he was concerned for her.

He wants to help me. Why should I allow it to bother me? Because she suspected that he disapproved of her, and she feared getting a lecture about acting like a proper young Amish woman.

She met his gaze as she climbed the steps. The way he stared at her gave her goose bumps.

"Afraid?" he asked softly.

"Of what?"

His expression filled with satisfaction. "Exactly. There is nothing to fear."

It was a clear autumn day with pleasant temperatures and sunshine. The house was silent, especially for Visiting Sunday. The warmer weather would soon be gone. Everyone preferred to enjoy these last days outdoors. As she glanced around the Peachy kitchen, Charlie raised a hand to tuck fine strands of hair under her prayer *kapp*. She became aware of Nate as never before.

He gestured toward a chair. "Sit," he ordered.

Annoyed, she lifted her chin.

"Please," he added softly.

She sat, willing to listen after he'd asked nicely.

He opened a kitchen cabinet and pulled out

a tube of ointment and a box of bandages. He set them on the table close to her before he reached into a drawer for a clean tea towel. He ran the sink, wet the cloth and returned to her. "Where exactly did you hurt yourself?"

She reached for the wet towel. "I can clean it." But he ignored her and hunkered down to wipe up the trail of blood. She blushed. She was barefoot and her feet were dirty, as were her legs from playing ball and sliding across the yard into home plate.

Nate was gentle as he washed her leg. He wiped up what he could see then looked up at her. "Here," he said, his voice husky. "You can clean the rest."

Charlie nodded and waited until he turned away to raise her dress just enough to reveal her scraped, bleeding knee. As the cloth touched the wound, she hissed out with pain. Nate spun and locked gazes with her. He glanced down then scowled at her. "Charlie Stoltzfus, look what you've done to yourself."

She stiffened and looked away, unwilling to see the condemnation in his eyes. "I had a home run."

"*Ja*, you did," he said with a chuckle that had her shooting him a startled gaze. "*Gut* job, by the way."

She gaped at him. He wasn't scolding her;

he was praising her. Stunned, she could only stare at him.

"You've dripped bloody water on the floor," he said gently. He reached and took the cloth from her then washed it under the faucet. "Are you hurt anywhere else?" he asked casually. She averted her glance, glad that he couldn't see the rising heat in her cheeks.

"I'm fine," she said too quickly.

He looked at her then, arched an eyebrow as he returned to her side with the washed cloth. "Charlie."

Her gaze pleaded with him. "I'm fine."

He observed her a long moment, his expression softening. "As long as you're sure."

She bobbed her head.

He towered over her, a tall man older by at least seven years. "Will you let me take care of your knee?" He regarded her kindly.

She drew a calming breath. *"Ja."*

"Gut girl."

She glared at him. *"Please.* I'm not a child."

He knelt and gently cleansed her knee and the lower half of her leg. He dried it with another clean cloth that she hadn't noticed he'd held. "What are you? All of sixteen?"

"I'll be nineteen in two weeks."

He seemed taken aback at her answer. She wasn't sure but she thought he'd murmured, "I had no idea." But he didn't look at her when he spoke. He was busy applying first-aid ointment before he covered her scrape with a bandage. "There you go," he said without expression. He reached for her arm and helped her to her feet.

"Danki," she murmured and quickly turned to leave, her arm tingling where he'd touched her. He didn't stop her from going. Charlie hurried outside to join her family for lunch. She didn't look back to see if Nate had left the house. She went right to the food table, grabbed a plate and helped herself. Spying her family at a table under a shade tree, she made her way over and sat down with a smile. If anyone wondered why it took so long for her to join them, they didn't mention it.

"*Gut* game, Charlie," Henry Yoder said as he set a plate in front of his wife then slid onto the bench next to her.

Charlie didn't say anything at first as she stared down at her plate. She should have been there to help the women. She'd been so focused on the game that she'd lost track of time. Now she felt guilty for not doing her share. She'd have to make sure she did most of the cleanup afterward.

"Charlie?"

She blinked and realized that her brother-in-law had spoken and she hadn't answered. "I'm sorry." She saw him eyeing her with concern. She managed a grin. "It was a *gut* game. Noah and Daniel aren't happy with me right now."

"*Ja*, but Joseph and I are."

She gave him a genuine smile. She really liked her sister Leah's husband. They'd been married a year, and her respect and liking of him had only grown. The fact that he made her sister ridiculously happy only heightened her feelings for him.

"You didn't hurt yourself when you fell, did you?"

She shook her head. "*Nay*, I'm fine. A little skinned knee is nothing when we got the win."

"Did you take care of it? Your knee?" her sister Leah asked with concern.

"All cleaned and bandaged." Fortunately, her family didn't question that she'd taken care of her injury. She looked down at her plate as she felt her face heat. She'd spent enough time in the Peachy house watching their youngest children that she knew where everything was kept.

She grew silent as Nate's tender first-aid ministration played on her mind. She caught sight of the man deep in conversation with his brother across the yard and felt a kick to her belly as his gaze brushed over her casually before he looked away.

"Do you think it's wrong of me to like playing baseball?" she asked no one in particular as she paused in her eating.

Her brother-in-law frowned. "*Nay*. Why?"

She shook her head. "It doesn't matter." Nathaniel Peachy didn't matter, she thought, but knew she was lying to herself to believe it.

Henry studied her a long moment, his expression softening. "You had fun, didn't you?"

She nodded.

"*Gut*, because we did, too, and we like having you on our team."

Charlie smiled. She started to eat, then froze when Nate slipped onto the far end of the bench at the next table. Why couldn't she get him out of her mind? The man was years older than she was, and she was more than a little fascinated by him. Which wasn't wise, she scolded herself. Not wise at all.

Nate studied Charlie and felt his stomach tighten. Charlie Stoltzfus had shown time and again to be a good ballplayer. Her focus couldn't be questioned. Every Sunday, whenever there was a game, the young men within their Amish community fought good-naturedly over which team would get Charlie.

He scowled. Good ballplayer or not, Charlie was too wild, too impulsive.

A lot like Emma.

A shaft of pain hit him hard, making his chest hurt with the memory of the girl he'd loved and lost. Emma had been wild and reckless, always searching for excitement. In the end, her wild behavior had led to her death.

Charlie Stoltzfus needed someone young but stable to keep her in check. Someone who could keep her safe and alive. Someone like... Nate glanced about the yard, searching for a prospective suitor for her, but he didn't find anyone suitable.

"Nate, aren't you going to eat?" his younger sister asked. Ruth Ann sat across the table from him.

He nodded as he flashed her a smile. "What are you having?"

"Roast beef and sides. And there are sandwiches if I'm still hungry."

"You love sandwiches." He recalled making them for her when she was much younger after his mother had died. He experienced a moment's sadness for a young life cut short too soon until he thought of his stepmother. *Mam* was as different from Charlie Stoltzfus

as night and day. She had made his father—
his whole family—happy. She was pregnant
again, due sometime in early January.

At his age, Nate never thought he'd have
a baby brother or sister. In fact, he'd hoped
that he'd be married with children of his own
by now. But he hadn't found the right woman
yet. Someone kind and loving who wanted the
same things from life as he did. There was
farm property down the road from his parents
he'd been hankering after. Once he acquired
the land, he'd be ready to find someone to
marry. Someone older and mature. Someone
unlike Charlie Stoltzfus.

Nate started to eat. He stilled with fork in
hand as he glanced toward the table where
Henry sat with his wife, Leah, and Charlie.
Her sister Nell and her husband, James, were
seated across from them.

"Aren't you hungry?" Ruth asked.

Desperate to ignore Charlie Stoltzfus, he
nodded at his sister then ate the food off his
fork. Unfortunately, he and Charlie faced each
other, and he found himself unable to keep
his eyes off her. She had beautiful features
with a pert little nose and pretty pink lips. Her
red-gold hair glistened brightly under the sun.
Her eyes were a deep shade of vivid green.

Her spring-green dress only heightened her coloring, highlighting her beauty.

He looked away. She was trouble, and he had to stop thinking about her.

"Charlie played a *gut* game today," his brother Jacob commented.

"She's got a lot of energy, that girl," his sister Mary Elizabeth said.

"She didn't help you with the food," Nate murmured and immediately regretted his comment.

Mam raised her eyebrows. "We had more than enough help. Take a look. Do you see a lack of women here? Charlie enjoys the game, but she would have come if we'd asked." Her speculative look made Nate squirm.

"I've never seen anyone hit the ball like she does," he said softly, sincerely, brushing the awkward moment aside. "She brought everyone on base home then slid into home plate, giving the team the win."

"*Ja*, I wish I could play like that," Ruth Ann said.

He blinked, but he didn't say a word. He waited for his father to comment, but the man only chuckled.

"You're much better off spending your time gardening," *Dat* said.

Nate breathed a sigh of relief. "*Ja*, gardening is a fine way to spend your time. Did you pick the last of the vegetables?"

"Plan to do it tomorrow," his sister said. "If there are any left. I haven't checked recently."

Ruth loved to garden so bringing up the subject was brilliant. He had to give his father credit. The man knew how to deal with his children in a way that was natural and loving without being overbearing.

Nate hoped that someday he could be the kind of father his *dat* was. And a leader like him. Some folks within his community thought that one day Nate would be asked to serve as deacon, preacher, or even bishop.

Nate closed his eyes. He hoped not. Being asked to serve as deacon would mean that his father had passed, for the position was lifelong. He didn't want to think of the day *Dat* was no longer with them. And he couldn't see himself as preacher or bishop. He could never live up to the title. Nate didn't feel good enough to be a church elder.

But he enjoyed farming. His father's farm wouldn't be his to inherit. The farm would go to his youngest brother, not the oldest son, as was the Amish way. Not that Nate minded. He would work for what he wanted. He had nearly enough money to bid on that other farm.

Charlie stood, immediately catching his attention.

He watched as she returned to the food table with her sisters Leah and Nell. They were chatting. Charlie laughed at something Nell said, and the change in her features was so startling that Nate was unable to look away. She was even more beautiful when she was happy. She'd always been a pretty little thing, but the way laughter changed her face stole his breath.

She was oblivious to his regard as she filled her dessert plate. He heard Leah chuckle and watched Charlie as she talked animatedly while gesturing with one hand, her movements nearly unseating the chocolate cake on her plate. The women kept up a steady conversation as they headed back to their table. Charlie giggled at something Leah said, but her good humor died quickly when she encountered his glance. Nell spoke and Charlie looked away, her smile restored. Awareness surged inside him. He recalled how he'd felt when he saw the blood on her leg. Anxiety. Anger. The strongest urge to protect her. He scowled. *I can't do this again.*

His chest tightened but he managed to eat

his lunch before heading to the dessert table with Ruth Ann. He didn't know why, but he was ready for the day to end.

"*Soohns*, we'll be leaving for Indiana first thing in the morning," his father said as Nate returned to the table. "I'd hoped the two of you would stay home and take care of things here."

Nate nodded. He'd known about his father's plans to take the family to see his grandparents. "We'll take care of the animals and make hay."

Jacob smiled. "Won't take us long."

"We'll take turns cooking," he warned his brother.

His brother shrugged. "I can survive on sandwiches."

He laughed. "I think you'll get sick of sandwiches, but we'll see."

After he finished eating, Nate rose to throw away his paper plate. He turned and caught a glimpse of Charlie standing at her cousin's paddock, watching the horses at play. Her glorious red hair was like a beacon that called to him. Why couldn't he stop thinking about her?

He headed in her direction.

Charlie gazed at the horses and felt a rush of pleasure. What she wouldn't give to race like the wind on the back of a horse! She smiled. The chestnut mare pranced and chased her companions into a playful gallop. She'd give anything to feel the freedom of riding through the fields with the warmth of the sun against her skin and her hair unpinned without a head covering. She closed her eyes and enjoyed the cool breeze tempered by the afternoon sunshine.

This week she wouldn't be babysitting for the youngest Peachy children. The family was going out of town, which made her sigh. She loved spending time with them and missed them when she wasn't needed. She loved children. It was her biggest wish to take over the teaching position at the Happiness School when the current schoolteacher left. That would be in a month or so, when current schoolteacher Elizabeth Troyer and her family moved to Ohio.

I'd make a gut *teacher.* She had done well in school, and she knew how to break down problems and find fun ways to make children remember what they'd learned. And she was ready. Her birthday was next month and she'd be nineteen. Her opportunity for teaching would be gone if it didn't happen soon. She planned to approach the church elders this week about her filling the upcoming vacancy.

The sun slipped beneath a cloud, and she felt a sudden chill. She hugged herself with her arms. The sky was only partially cloudy. In a few moments the sun would resurface and warm her again.

"Charlie."

She stiffened, recognizing his voice. She faced him. "Nate." The shock of his appearance made her heart flutter. Ironically, she'd come here alone to seek refuge from the feelings he'd churned up inside her.

He leaned against the fence rail with only a few inches separating them. She became instantly aware of the heat his nearness generated. Something within her urged to flee from him; yet, she didn't move.

She straightened her spine and stared. "What do you want, Nate? What are you doing here?"

"How's your knee?" he asked, his eyes soft with concern.

She swallowed hard. "Fine. Your first aid helped." She bit her lip. *"Danki."*

He nodded with satisfaction. "You like to play ball."

Charlie drew away, putting several more inches between them. *"Ja,* so?"

A tiny smile hovered on his lips. "You play well."

"Then why were you trying to distract me?"

"My *bruder* was on the other team."

She gaped at him for several seconds then laughed. She watched as his mouth curved into a grin before he joined in her laughter.

It felt good to laugh, yet strange to laugh with him. The fact that she liked the feeling made her stop laughing. Suddenly tense, she quieted and leaned against the fence and returned to her study of the horses.

They stood silently for a few moments. "What do you hope for, Charlie?" he asked. "In your life."

She hesitated. "I like children. I'd like to teach."

Clearly surprised, Nate raised his eyebrows. "You want to teach at our Happiness School?"

"Ja," she whispered. "I know there are some members within our community who won't think I'm good enough—"

"I believe you'd be an excellent teacher."

"You do?"

"Ja, I do." His gaze seemed intense as he studied her.

"What is it?" she asked.

"You surprise me." He paused, looking thoughtful. "I can help you."

"Help me what?"

"Become a teacher. My father is deacon. I could speak with him."

"Nay!" she gasped. "You mustn't."

"Why not?"

"I don't want or deserve the job if I can't earn it on my own."

He shook his head as he watched her, as if he'd learned something new about her that stunned him.

"Charlie!"

She glanced back to see Ellie waving at her. "Time to head home. I've got to go," she told Nate. "I—ah—*danki* again for helping me today."

"You're *willkomm.*"

"I'll see you next Sunday," she said.

Nate nodded without saying a word, and Charlie turned and hurried toward their buggy, where her family had gathered to leave.

Her heart hammered within her chest. Nate Peachy was a complex man, and she didn't understand him. With one breath, he'd told her she'd be a good teacher, but then in the next, he'd proven that he didn't believe it unless he stepped in to help. She sighed with sadness. If Nate felt this way, then there was every chance that no one would consider her seriously for the soon-to-be vacated teaching position. *Maybe I'm being foolish to try.*

When she was younger, her tendency to be impulsive frequently got her into trouble, but she was older and wiser now and she'd learned from her mistakes. She'd meant what she'd told Nate. If she couldn't get the job on her own, then she didn't want—or deserve—it.

Chapter Two

As his family left for Indiana, Nate watched the hired car that carried them until the vehicle disappeared from sight. He turned toward the house and saw his brother on the front porch, gazing after the car as if he, too, was affected by their departure.

Nate strode toward the house and climbed the porch steps. "Ready to make hay?"

"How about some breakfast first?" Jacob suggested.

"Didn't you eat earlier?"

"*Nay*, busy helping our sisters with their luggage."

He smiled with amusement. "You, too? I helped *Mam*, *Dat* and Harley with theirs."

The brothers headed inside for coffee and freshly baked muffins.

"I spoke with John King. His *dat* is lend-ing us his hay mower for as long as we need it," Jacob said as he finished up his coffee a while later.

"It will make the job easier." He eyed his brother with approval. "Do we need to go get it?"

"*Nay.* John said he'd bring it by first thing. He should be here anytime now."

Amos King, John's father, was also his stepmother's *dat*. He was a good man with a kind heart.

Nate washed the breakfast dishes while Jacob put the remaining muffins back in the pantry. The sound of horse hooves drew them outside to discover John King's arrival with the mower.

After John left with his brother Joshua, Nate hitched his father's two black Belgian horses to his *dat*'s equipment for his brother to use. He would mow the front field with Amos's mower while Jacob started work at the back of the property.

It was a busy workday. By late afternoon they'd mowed just over a third of the hay-fields. He and Jacob put away the mowers. They ate leftovers for dinner, before heading to the barn to make sure all of the animals were settled in for the night.

There was a definite new chill in the

air when Nate arose the next morning. He dressed, made coffee and waited for his brother to rouse and join him. The kitchen filled with the rich scent of the perked brew as Jacob entered, looking sleepy-eyed with tousled hair.

"'Tis colder today. We'd best grab our woolen hats and jackets before we head out."

Jacob nodded as he turned from the stove with a mug of coffee. "Think we'll finish today?"

"We'll be pushing it. Didn't get much more than a third done yesterday."

His brother agreed. "We can do it."

Nate smiled. "We can try." The mowed hay would be left to dry in the fields before they baled it.

"Let's move," Jacob said as he set his mug in the sink.

Charlie drove down the road toward Whittier's Store. It was a chilly November morning, but she didn't mind. She wore her black bonnet and woolen cape with a heavy blanket across her lap. Her mother's list was on the seat beside her with the apple pie *Mam* had baked for Leah and Henry. She would stop first at Yoder's Country Crafts and Supplies, her sister Leah's shop, to deliver the pie before continuing on to grocery-shop.

The sunshine was bright across the surrounding farmland. A farmer cut hay in the fields ahead and she watched him as she steered her horse closer. The man maneuvered his horse-drawn mower down the length of the hayfield before turning to mow the uncut section.

Charlie smiled. She knew how to use a mower. With five daughters and no sons, her father had been glad of her help, once she'd convinced him that she could handle the job. *Dat* had objected the first time, until her repeated requests made him finally relent enough to show her how. She'd been pleased by his smile of approval after she'd mowed in neat, even rows across their field. After that he'd allowed her to relieve him while he'd completed other chores.

It had been a while since she'd mowed hay. Watching the farmer work made her smile and long for another chance on the back of a mower.

She returned her attention to the road. She had gone only a short distance when she heard someone bellow sharply in alarm. Startled, she drew up on the reins to stop her horse. Her heart went cold when she saw that the mower had tipped and the farmer lay on the ground. A second man raced toward the fallen farmer, and with a gasp, she recognized Nate Peachy. She pulled her vehicle off the road and secured her horse before she sprinted across the field to help.

She briefly locked gazes with Nate before she turned her attention to the man on the ground—his brother Jacob. "Jake, are you hurt?" she rasped, out of breath.

"Charlie." Jacob met her gaze and smiled. "I'm fine." But when he tried to stand, he cried out with pain and fell back.

Nate's brow creased with worry. "Stay still. You are *not* fine."

Charlie hunkered beside the injured man and experienced the impact of Nate's startling blue gaze. She glanced away. "What hurts?" she and Nate asked simultaneously.

"My foot."

"Can you walk?" Nate asked.

"I don't know. I don't think so."

"My buggy is right there," Charlie said, gesturing. "Maybe we can lift him into it…" She bit her lip as Nate rose. He stared down at her thoughtfully until she stood. "I can bring it closer." She returned her attention to the man's brother. "Jake?"

"I can make it with help."

Her gaze met Nate's. "Where do you want me to park it?"

"Leave it," he said sharply. "Your vehicle is fine where it is." He narrowed his eyes. "Go back there and wait. I'll bring Jacob."

Unwilling to argue, Charlie stood by her buggy and waited. Jacob gave her a weak smile as the brothers approached. The young man was obviously in pain, and she worried about him. Nate bore the brunt of Jacob's weight as he half carried him with an arm securely around his brother's waist.

She wondered how to help, but knew instinctively that Nate would mutter something cutting if she tried. Charlie watched silently as he lifted his brother into the back of the buggy.

"We should get him to the clinic."

Nate flashed her an irritated look. "*I'll* take him after I see to the horses and equipment. Drive around to the front of the *haus*," he ordered. "I'll meet you there."

His tone irritated her. She had to bite her tongue to keep from arguing with him. "I can take care of the horses and equipment for you."

"*Nay,*" he snapped. "Absolutely not."

Charlie reeled back, offended. "I know how

to handle farm equipment, Nathaniel Peachy. I've mowed hay for my *vadder*."

"I don't want you touching *ours*, Charlotte Stoltzfus. If you want to help, then get my *bruder* back to the house. I'll meet you there."

"Fine," she agreed as she abruptly turned away. She didn't bother to look to see what Nate was doing as she climbed into the buggy and checked on Jacob. "How're you doing, Jake?"

"Foot hurts, but I'll live."

She frowned. "What happened?"

"I got distracted." He seemed embarrassed.

She flicked the leathers and the horse moved. "What distracted you?"

"I don't know. One minute I was mowing and the next I felt a sudden jerk on the reins. It threw me off balance."

"Do you see any blood?"

She heard Jacob take in a breath. *"Nay."*

She shot him a glance over her shoulder before she returned her attention to the road. "Do you feel like you're bleeding?"

"My foot feels odd. I could be, I guess, but I can't tell for sure. I don't think so."

Charlie sighed with relief. *"Gut.* That's *gut."* She could only hope that he wasn't. She knew what could happen if farm equipment tipped over. Injuries could be as mild as simple bumps and bruises to severe loss of limb or life.

It took ten minutes or more for her to drive to the Abram Peachy house. She pulled her vehicle onto the dirt drive and parked close to the barn just as Nate exited the building. At his approach, Charlie experienced a constriction in her chest.

"Hold on a minute, and I'll move him into our buggy," he told her as he drew near.

"Use mine. There's no need to move him." She hesitated. "You might aggravate his injury."

He sighed. "You're probably right."

It was clear that the last thing Nate wanted was for her to accompany them. "I'll wait for you here," she said quietly.

Something dark briefly crossed across his features. "The house is unlocked. You can warm up inside. Make yourself tea or something." He paused. "You know where everything is kept." And that bothered him, she realized.

Nate stepped back and waited for her to climb down. She watched as he got onto the seat she'd vacated before switching her attention to Jacob in the back. "You still *oll recht* in there, Jake?"

Jacob's face was whiter than it had been earlier, but he nodded.

"Don't worry. The doctor will fix you right up." She gave him a reassuring smile. "I'll see you when you get back."

"I don't know how long this will take," Nate said. "We could be gone awhile. Are you sure you don't want me to move him so you can have your buggy and leave?"

"*Nay.* There is no place I have to be." She stepped back and waited for them to leave.

Nate suddenly glanced down. "You've an apple pie in here." He speared her with his gaze as he lifted it for her to see.

She shrugged then approached to get it. "I was going to take it to Leah, but she doesn't know. I'll bring it in and you both can have a piece when you get back."

Nate handed her the pie through the open window along with her shopping list. "Pie smells *gut.*" He gave her a twisted smile. "Did you make it?"

She stiffened. "*Nay, Mam* did." She knew instantly what he thought—that the pie wouldn't be edible if she'd made it. His look of disappointment surprised. "You should get going. Jacob doesn't look well at all."

Charlie watched until the vehicle was out of sight before she returned to the house with the apple pie. She debated whether or not to make tea, as Nate had suggested. But then she thought of the fields yet to be mowed and the forecast for rain for the next few days and she headed toward the barn instead. Without thought, she readied the smaller of the two mowers. It wouldn't take her long to finish the work that Jacob had started.

As she climbed onto the seat and urged the horses forward, she thought of Nate. He'd be upset with her for doing what he'd considered a man's job. She drew in and released a sharp breath. The benefit of a job well-done was worth risking Nate's anger. Once he realized how efficient she was in cutting hay, he'd be glad to see that she'd mowed a substantial amount of ground.

The task went smoothly. Charlie enjoyed herself as she worked to finish the back section of Abram Peachy's farm. Time flew by and she realized that she'd been out longer than she'd expected. She stabled the horses and left the mower right where she'd found it.

There was no sign of her buggy in the yard as she headed back to the house. Her relief was short-lived as she became concerned about Jacob. The brothers had been gone a long while. Was Jacob that badly hurt?

Charlie put on the teakettle then set the

table with the pie in the center. She made a fresh pot of coffee with the hope that the brothers would return soon enough to enjoy a hot cup. When she was done, she stepped outside. As the buggy pulled into the yard and parked near the house, she descended the porch steps.

"How is he?" she asked as Nate climbed out of the vehicle.

"He broke his foot," Nate told her. "There's a nice-size slice in it, too, which the doc stitched up." He reached in to lift Jacob into his arms. "He's been advised to stay off the foot for a while." His brother looked groggy as Nate carried him toward the house.

Charlie raced ahead to open the door. She made a sound of concern at Jacob's pallor.

"The doctor gave him a shot of pain medication," Nate explained as he carried Jacob inside.

"Do you need help?"

"I can manage." He shifted Jacob within his arms and brought him into the kitchen.

When she saw Nate looking for a place to set Jacob down, she rushed to pull out a chair. "Unless you want to take him into the great room."

"I'd like to sit here a bit," Jacob murmured

sleepily. "Do I smell coffee? And what about that pie you promised us?"

She fretted as she studied him. "Jake, you don't look good. Wouldn't you rather lie down?"

"*Nay.* I will soon, though." Jacob frowned up at his older brother, who stepped back after setting him down. "I'll be of no help to you for a while, I'm afraid."

"I'll manage," Nate assured him.

Charlie felt her throat tighten as she went to the stove. "Nate, do you want coffee, too?" she asked easily, pretending that she wasn't upset by the morning's events.

"*Ja,* please." Nate took the chair next to his brother, as if he wanted to keep a close eye on him.

She could feel Nate's gaze as she poured two cups of hot coffee then set one before each man. "Apple pie, or do you want a sandwich first?"

Nate's study of her made her self-conscious. "Pie will do."

Her lips curved slightly as she nodded. Charlie cut two large slices of apple pie.

"Aren't you having any? Or do you have to leave?" Nate asked as she pushed a plate in his direction.

"I should go," she said, stung by the question. "But I won't until after I have some pie." He looked amused when she gave him a false smile.

It was quiet as they ate. Glad when Nate didn't make a smart remark, Charlie glanced from her plate to Jacob, who slumped in his chair. She was about to express her worry to Nate then caught him studying his brother with a frown.

"Time to rest, *bruder*," Nate said gently. "Let's get you into the other room where you'll be more comfortable."

While they were absent, Charlie quickly cleaned up the kitchen. She covered the remainder of the pie with plastic wrap and left it on the counter for them to finish later. She washed the dishes but left the coffeepot on the stove in case Nate wanted another cup.

She felt his presence as Nate reentered the room and sensed him watching while she put away the last dish.

"He settled in?" she asked, turning to face him.

"*Ja*, he's already asleep."

"I'm going to head out. I need to pick up a few things at the store for my *mudder*."

He eyed her with consternation. "We've kept you a long time."

"'Tis fine. *Mam* doesn't expect me home

yet. She'll think that I decided to spend the day with Leah."

"You had an unusual day today," he said.

She chuckled. "That's for sure."

He sobered. "It wasn't fair to ask you to stay."

"I didn't mind."

He seemed relieved. He followed her as she headed toward the door. "Charlie? May I ask you one more favor?"

She halted and faced him. "*Ja*, of course." He seemed to have difficulty choosing his words.

"What do you need, Nate?" By the look on his face, she figured out what he wanted to ask. "Shall I come to stay with Jacob tomorrow while you cut hay?"

Nate released a sharp breath. "You wouldn't mind?"

She paused near the threshold. "Not at all."

Warmth entered his blue eyes. "Are you sure?"

Feigning annoyance, she tapped her foot and crossed her arms. "I'm absolutely sure, Nate."

"*Danki.*" His expression became serious. "But I need you to promise that you won't tell anyone what happened," he said. "You know that our neighbors like to natter." His lips firmed. "Especially Alta Hershberger. If she or anyone finds out, word could get back to my *eldre*, and *Dat* will insist on cutting short their trip." He paused. "He's been waiting a long time to visit my grandparents. I don't want to ruin his plans."

"I understand," she murmured. "If anyone asks why I'm here, I'll tell them I'm cleaning house for you while you work in the fields."

"Doesn't your sister Ellie clean houses?"

"*Ja*, but I've spent enough time in your house helping your *mam* that it makes sense that I be the one to do it."

His expression was unreadable. "Appreciate it."

"I'd do the same for any neighbor," she assured him.

He accompanied her outside. "Drive safely, Charlie," he said sternly.

Annoyed, she nodded before she climbed into her buggy and drove away. She didn't mind coming back the next day. Nate would be busy and she wouldn't have to see or talk with him for long. She would be there for Jacob, the easygoing, much younger and friendlier Peachy brother.

Still, as she drove toward Whittier's Store to buy the items on her mother's list, she couldn't help but think about Nate and wonder why she felt so drawn to the man. At times he treated her like a child, and she hated it. But then there were those other occasions when he studied her differently, as if he saw her as a woman, an attractive woman he found fascinating.

Charlie sighed as she stored the bought groceries onto the seat next to her. She was imagining things. Nate didn't find her attractive or pretty or anything good.

She would get through tomorrow then concentrate on getting hired on as the new teacher for their Happiness School. Better to focus on that than on her disturbing fascination with Nathaniel Peachy.

Chapter Three

Charlie stared at the cups and dishes that she'd left on the table after fixing Jacob and Nate breakfast then worked to clean up. Nate had left for the fields. She had given Jacob his pain medicine and he was in the great room, resting on the sofa.

Dishes cleaned and put away, she turned her attention to the time. Would Nate come in for lunch? He didn't say.

Nate had seemed relieved to see her that morning, but he'd said little except in appreciation of the food she'd prepared for him and Jacob.

With breakfast done, she found herself at loose ends. Now what? What should she do now?

Charlie grinned. She'd clean the house from top to bottom. The brothers' *mam* would be surprised to see a clean house when only her sons were in residence.

She'd hung up the wet tea towel she'd used to dry dishes when suddenly the back door slammed open. She gasped and spun to see a furious man. "Nate? What's wrong?"

"Charlie Stoltzfus," he snapped, "did you take out the mower yesterday while Jacob and I were at the doctor?"

Charlie flushed guiltily and glanced away. "I wanted to help."

"And I told you to stay away from the equipment!" he burst out.

"I know how to mow hay!"

He approached, grabbed her roughly by the shoulders, but despite his intimidating height and expression, he didn't hurt her and she wasn't afraid. "You saw what happened to Jacob yesterday," he said. His eyes were like blue ice. "What if you'd been hurt while we were gone? Who would have been here to help you?" He released her and stepped back. He turned away. Tension tightened the muscles of his back, and he clenched his fists at his sides. He spun to face her. "People die in farm accidents, Charlie!"

Guilt made her flush. She felt a painful lump in her throat. "You're right," she said. "I'm sorry."

Nate held her gaze. He looked big and handsome—and extremely upset.

"I'm sorry I used the mower without your permission." She drew a sharp breath then released it. "I wanted to help. 'Tis supposed to rain soon and I knew you'd be missing a day's work with Jacob's accident yesterday. I thought if I finished what he'd started there would be less for you to worry about." She fought back tears. Charlie shifted uncomfortably when he just stared at her. "Say something," she said.

"You want to be *schuul*teacher," he said harshly. "You have to think before you act, Charlie. Your behavior frequently gets you into trouble. How can you teach our community children if you jump into situations without giving a thought to the consequences?"

She felt the blood leave her face. "You don't think I'd be a *gut* teacher."

He sighed and approached her. "You need to be more careful. To grow up." He placed his hands gently on her arms then soothed them down their length to take her hands. "I think you could be a fine teacher. You have a way with children. They listen to you and will gladly follow your lead." He released her abruptly, his expression hardening. "But you won't be teacher unless you can lead them by *gut* example. You have to stop jumping rashly into situations that can potentially be dangerous."

"I know how to mow," she insisted, stung. "And you refer to things I did as a child."

He shifted away and crossed the room. "Maybe you do know how to mow. It doesn't matter," he said sharply. "I told you to stay away from the mowers and you didn't. *Gut* intentions don't make it right." He leaned against the wall near the door. "And you acted like a child. A spoiled, disobedient child."

"You're not my *vadder*!" she yelled.

"Thank the Lord for that."

Blinking sleepily, Jacob appeared in the doorway, clutching the door frame as he wobbled on one foot. "What's going on?"

Nate studied his brother. "What are you doing up? If you fall, you'll do further damage to yourself."

"I thought I heard arguing." The younger man glanced from her to his brother and back.

Charlie blushed. "We were just…"

"Having a serious discussion," Nate said. His lips firmed. "She mowed hay yesterday while we were gone."

Jacob glanced at her with surprise. "You did?"

Charlie hesitated then inclined her head. "I know how to mow. I've done it for my *dat*."

Nate's brother grinned. "How much did you get done?"

"I finished the back acreage where you left off and a little more."

"Don't," Nate warned Jacob. "Don't encourage her. You know what can happen when an accident occurs with the mower. She could have been hurt or worse."

His expression sobering, Jacob gazed at her. "He's right."

She lifted her chin defiantly. "Maybe."

Nate stared at his brother. "Jake, you need to lie down before you fall."

To Charlie's surprise, Jacob agreed. She moved to help him into the other room, but Nate reached him first. As if he didn't trust her to help Jacob. Hurt, she stayed in the kitchen while the brothers disappeared into the other room. While she waited for Nate to return, she felt the strongest urge to flee. But she didn't. She might have made a huge mistake with the mower, but she was just trying to help. Charlie still thought he'd overacted, and she wouldn't run as if she'd done something wrong.

But she didn't want him to think her unreliable and immature. She wanted the teaching job and needed to show him that she was a dependable, no-nonsense young woman who would make the best teacher ever hired for their Happiness School. A wrong word from Nate or anyone else within the community would end her chances to teach. As much as it upset her to change, she understood she needed to be on her best behavior. Even if it killed her to change into someone other than herself.

After making sure Jacob was comfortable on the sofa, Nate returned to the kitchen. He paused in the doorway, his gaze immediately homing in on Charlie. She stared out the window over the sink. There was a defeated slump to her shoulders, and he could feel her dejection like pain in his belly. But as much as it hurt him to see her this way, he knew he was right to be hard on her.

He stepped into the room. "Charlie."

She spun as if taken by surprise. A look of vulnerability settled on her pretty features. He scowled. He didn't want to notice how lovely she was or to recall her misguided intentions to help. If she didn't rein in her tendency to jump into potentially dangerous situations, she could get seriously injured. Or die.

Her breath shuddered out. "Jacob *oll recht*?"

"*Ja.* He's asleep."

Her mouth softened into a slight smile. "The pain medication."

He nodded, unable to take his gaze off her. He'd been more than a little alarmed when he'd realized that she'd used the mower. If something had happened to her...

A memory came to him sharp and painful of another young girl who'd been reckless and wild like Charlie. He'd loved Emma with all of the love in a young boy's heart, but it hadn't been enough. Despite his repeated warnings, Emma had continued to take risks in her quest for excitement. She'd claimed that she loved him, but in the end, he wasn't enough to keep her happy. He'd warned her to avoid the young *Englishers* in town, but she hadn't listened.

Instead, she'd called him a spoilsport for ruining her fun. Then one night she'd slipped out of the house during her *rumspringa* to spend time with her new English friends. The teenage driver had crashed his car, the accident seriously wounding his passengers, three English girls, and killing Emma immediately.

Nate hadn't known of Emma's plans that night. Later in his grief, he'd realized that Emma would have hated being married to an Amish farmer. Never content to be a wife and a mother, she would have always craved—and gone looking for—excitement.

Charlie shifted uncomfortably under his gaze and he looked away. Charlie needed a husband, he thought. A man to ground her. Someone closer to her age with enough sense to help her reach her potential as a responsible wife and mother.

"Charlie—"

"I only wanted to help, Nathaniel," she said.

He stifled a smile at the use of his formal given name. She tended to use it whenever she was upset with him. "I know."

"But I didn't, did I? I made you worry and I didn't mean to."

He sighed. "Next time you need to listen when I tell you something."

"I guess that will depend on what you say," she said cheekily.

"Charlie," he warned.

"I'm not a child, and I can only be me."

"I need to get back to work," he said abruptly. He had to maintain his distance. He mustn't think of her as anything other than a child.

"Will you be back for lunch?"

He hesitated. "I'm not sure. If I am, most likely I'll be late. If the two of you get hungry, eat." He grabbed his hat from the table where he'd tossed it earlier. "I need to stay out and cut as much hay as possible before it rains."

An odd sound made him spin around. Charlie looked as if she was going to say something but she didn't.

Nate studied her face and had to stifle amusement at the aggrieved look in her green eyes. "Stay in the *haus*, Charlie. Jacob needs you."

She sniffed as if he'd found fault with her. "I'll keep an eye on him."

He didn't release her gaze. *"Gut."* Jamming his hat on his head, he opened the back door and took one last look to find her reaching for the broom. "Charlie."

She spun as if startled. *"Ja?"*

"Behave."

She glared at him. "Go mow your hay, *vadder*," she mocked.

Nate chuckled under his breath as he left, pulling the door shut behind him. He was overly conscious that Charlie was in his home, doing her best to help out in a bad situation. He didn't know what he would have done if she hadn't been there yesterday.

He gauged the sky, noting the gathering dark clouds in the far distance. The last thing he needed was for it to rain before he was done.

He couldn't dawdle. Time was passing too

quickly, and he'd already spent too much of it at the house when he should have been in the fields. But after realizing what Charlie had done, he hadn't been able to stay away.

Nate scowled. Lately, Charlie was taking up way too many of his thoughts. She wanted to be a teacher. Maybe that was just what she needed—a job to keep her busy and that would make her take responsibility more seriously. His *mam* frequently sang Charlie's praises for the way she handled his younger siblings. *Mam* obviously felt Charlie responsible enough to watch her children while she did other things.

He had a ton of work to do, Nate reminded himself. He forced Charlie from his mind to focus on the task at hand.

Four hours later he was pleased to realize that he'd cut more acreage than expected. He hated to admit it, but Charlie's work in the back fields the previous morning had helped him. As he stabled his Belgian team, he felt the first of the rain. He closed the barn door then headed to the house, his thoughts immediately returning to Charlie and the lunch she'd promised him.

Nate was overwhelmed with a sudden chill as the rain began to fall in earnest, soaking him. As he reached the house, the door opened and Charlie stood, studying him with a worried look. "'Tis raining," she said, eyeing him carefully, noting his soaked clothes.

Nate nodded. "I know." Water dripped from his straw hat onto the porch decking. He tugged off his hat, and his hair underneath was sopping. The hat had done nothing to keep out the rain. She held out her hand for the hat then stepped back so he could enter the house. He followed her with his gaze. "You were worried."

She looked away, apparently unwilling to admit concern. "I made soup," she said.

He let it go. "Sounds *gut*." He shivered. "And hot." He smiled. "I need warming up."

"You should change into dry garments," she suggested.

He spun toward her. "Is that an order?"

"It would help." She blinked. "And it was just an idea."

He grinned, silently laughing at her. "'Tis a *gut* one." He started across the kitchen toward the hall to the stairs. He halted and faced her. "How's Jacob?"

"Seems *oll recht*. He's resting. In fact, he's been sleeping most of the morning. He woke up about an hour ago and I made him tea, but I think he's fallen asleep again."

"He needs his rest." He turned to leave.

"Nathaniel."

He spun back. *"Ja?"*

"Did you finish the mowing?"

"I did."

She looked relieved. *"Gut.* I'll check on Jacob then put the soup on the table."

"What kind of soup?" he asked, curious.

"Ham and lima bean."

His favorite. *Humph.* Was she aware? He studied her a moment. *Nay,* he decided, eyeing her with approval. So she could make soup. What else could she cook? He needed to know if he was to find her a husband. *After I help her to get the teaching position at our Happiness School.*

Jacob opened his eyes as Charlie entered the room. "How are you feeling?" she asked softly.

"Like someone slashed my foot with a sickle."

"I'm sorry," she said with genuine sympathy. "Is there anything I can do to help?"

"Nay." He gave her a small smile. "I'll live but *danki."*

"Are you hungry? Nate's back." She'd been sick with relief when he'd walked, dripping wet, into the house. She'd fretted all morning, wondering if the mower had overturned and pinned him beneath metal.

"Nate's home?"

She shook off the mental image. "*Ja.* 'Tis raining. He's changing into dry clothes." She waited patiently as he sat up. "Can I help you into the kitchen?"

"*Nay.* I need to talk with him first," he said gruffly. "You go. We'll be there in a few minutes."

Not understanding why Jacob's comment stung her, Charlie returned to the kitchen. She set out bowls, napkins and silverware. She sliced the loaf of bread she'd found earlier in the pantry and cut up a block of cheddar in case they wanted a sandwich.

Nate entered alone moments later as she debated whether or not anything was missing from the table. She knew the exact second he entered the room.

"Did Jacob eat?" he asked.

"*Nay.* He'll join us, but said he wants to talk with you first." She watched Nate's brow furrow before he left to check on his brother.

He was gone a long time. Now that he was home, there was no need for her to stay. She would eat, then clean up before taking her leave.

Nate entered, his arm supporting Jacob.

He helped him to the table and pulled out a chair. Charlie adjusted the seat opposite for Jake to use as a footrest.

"The soup smells *gut*." Nate grabbed the chair next to his brother. "I'm starved. How about you, Jake?"

Looking pale, Jacob didn't answer.

Charlie frowned. "You don't like ham and bean soup, Jake?"

"I like it well enough. I don't feel much like eating."

"I can heat up a can of chicken soup. There's one in the pantry."

"Nay," Jacob said with a genuine smile. "I'll have a cup of the ham and bean."

Charlie ladled the soup into a large tureen and placed it in the center of the table. She held out her hand for Nate's bowl. His gaze locked on her as he gave it to her. The intensity of his look made her face heat. She hoped he'd believe it was from the hot soup rather than from her reaction to him. She set a filled bowl carefully before him then reached to fill a cup for Jacob. "Would you like bread, Jake?" she asked. "If your stomach is upset, it may help."

He looked surprised but nodded. Charlie passed him the bread plate and butter dish. Jacob reached for a slice and buttered it.

"Don't I get bread, too?" Nate teased.

She felt suddenly flustered until she realized that he was giving her a hard time simply because he could. A little imp inside made her cheeky. "*Ja.* Jacob, pass your *bruder* the bread plate, please."

Nate continued to watch her. Her stomach reacted when he gave her a slow smile. She looked away, filled her soup bowl then sat down across from Nate.

The men expressed appreciation for her cooking, and Charlie felt inordinately pleased by their praise. She ate her soup slowly, not wanting to rush and spill it. The brothers discussed the farmwork to be done once the rain stopped.

"I need to fix the leak in our storage building roof," Nate said.

"Can't you just bale it into rolls and cover them in plastic to leave outside?" Charlie asked. Many Amish farmers within her community stored hay that way.

Surprisingly, it was Jacob who looked at her as if she were an oddity.

Nate calmly explained why they chose to bale the hay into blocks instead. They would lay plastic over the top of the stack to protect them from the weather until they could move the hay inside. "'Tis easier to store.

Hay wrapped too long in plastic can ferment. Feeding fermented hay to our animals can make them tipsy. *Dat* doesn't like to use fermented hay."

"My *vadder* has used rolled hay bales." She paused. "I have seen tipsy cows on occasion."

Nate regarded her patiently. "Many use rolled bales successfully, but my *vadder* isn't one of them."

The men finished eating. Charlie ate the last of her soup then stood to clear the table. Nate rose and helped Jacob into the other room. He returned within moments as she stacked dirty dishes on the counter near the sink. "You have plenty of soup left for another meal," she said as she ran hot water into a dish basin. When he didn't comment, she faced him. "Is something wrong?" She sighed with disappointment. "The soup didn't taste *gut*." Dismayed, she began to wash dishes.

"It was delicious," he assured her as he approached. To her shock, he pulled out a dish towel and started to dry the dishes.

"I'm glad you liked it." She grew silent. "You don't have to dry dishes."

"I want to. Like you, I don't mind helping others."

She didn't know how to respond. Was he

mocking her? "Is that a subtle reminder of what I've done wrong?"

"Nay." He continued to work in silence.

She was conscious of him working beside her, the way his big hands handled the bowl carefully as he ran the towel over its surface. As he dried each one, Nate stacked them on the countertop near the cabinet where they'd be put away.

She needed to leave, she thought. Being this close to Nate made her uneasy.

"Now that you're here, I'll leave once I'm done here."

She felt him tense up. "Will you come back tomorrow?"

"You want me to?" she asked with surprise.

"I need someone to stay with Jacob," he said without warmth. "Tomorrow I'll be working with Jed."

Charlie closed her eyes briefly. When she opened them, it was to find Nate staring at her strangely with dish in hand. "I'll send one of my sisters if I can't make it. Either way, *Mam* needs to know."

"That's fine. But make sure she understands that no one else can know. My *dat* has waited a long time for this trip. If anyone accidentally lets the news slip when he calls to leave a message, he'll insist on coming home."

After the leftover food was put away and the kitchen cleaned, Charlie reached for her coat by the back door. "I'm heading out," she said.

"Danki." The intent focus of his blue eyes gave her goose bumps.

She lifted her coat only to feel it taken from her hands. Nate held it open for her so she could slide an arm into each sleeve. Then, to her shock, she felt his hands briefly settle on her shoulders before she'd pulled the garment closed. Pulse racing, she avoided his gaze. "Tell Jake I hope he feels better."

"I will." There was an odd huskiness to Nate's voice that she'd never heard before. He eyed her with an expression that made the back of her neck tingle as she met his gaze.

She cleared her throat. "I'll make sure someone is here for him tomorrow morning."

"Fine." He accompanied her to the door.

"What time?"

"Eight? Jed will be here at eight thirty."

She nodded. "Someone will be here before then."

"Be careful," he said, seemingly unmoved

by the knowledge that she wouldn't be the one coming. "The roads can be slippery when wet."

Charlie didn't respond, although she could have argued that she'd driven in the rain hundreds of times without any problems. She donned her traveling bonnet before she dashed outside. She sensed that Nate was behind her. She spun to face him. "*Nay*, go back inside! You'll get wet again."

She didn't wait to see if he listened. She climbed inside her vehicle, picked up the leathers, then left without another look. Her thoughts were in turmoil as she steered the horse toward home. She'd ask Ellie if she could stay with Jacob. If Ellie wasn't available, she'd ask Meg or Nell.

Tomorrow she'd speak with the bishop about becoming teacher. She couldn't avoid it any longer. It was time to get her life in order. Her sudden desire wasn't because the thought of seeing Nate so soon again thoroughly unnerved her.

Or was it?

Charlie released a sharp breath, all too aware of Nate's negative view of her. She'd prove that she was the perfect woman for the teaching job, and that her students would benefit from her instruction. Not that it really mattered what Nate thought, unless it affected or hurt her chances in getting the position.

Chapter Four

Nate glanced at the time and grew worried. *Where is she?* He had to leave shortly and Charlie promised that she or her sister would be here by now. Had he been wrong to trust her to keep her word? He recalled everything she'd done for Jacob and knew that there must be a good reason no one had arrived.

He entered the great room, where Jacob sat in a chair with his injured foot propped up on a stool. "Charlie isn't here yet," he told his brother. "Will you be *oll recht* until she arrives?"

Jacob glanced up from his book. "Charlie's late?" he asked with concern.

"*Ja.* But it might not be Charlie who's staying with you today. She said that one of her sisters might come in her place."

Alarm settled on his brother's features. "Something must have happened."

Jacob's comment intensified his fear. "Jed will be here any minute." Nate prayed that Charlie arrived before Jed did. He swallowed hard. He prayed that Charlie was well and not lying hurt in a ditch somewhere.

There was a loud rap on the back door and then he heard Charlie's voice call out, *"Hallo?"*

"We're in here," he called back. He stifled the urge to run to her and waited instead for her to come to them.

She entered, looking lovely, flushed and out of breath. "I'm sorry I'm late. I didn't have the use of a vehicle this morning, so I walked."

Nate stared at her, aware of how pretty she was. "You walked?" he asked with disbelief.

Charlie nodded. *"Ja."*

"Isn't that three miles?" Jacob asked with appreciation.

Charlie shrugged. "More like four. Doesn't matter. I told you someone would be here, and so here I am. A little late, and I'm sorry about that."

Nate felt something inside him warm. "You're here now and that's what counts." He caught a glimpse through the window of a horse-drawn wagon pulling into the yard. "Jed's here." He met Charlie's gaze. "Are you sure you're okay?"

She nodded. "A little winded because I was in a hurry, but otherwise I'm fine."

Despite the fact that Jed waited, he hesitated. The sudden stark need to spend time with her startled him.

"Did you eat?" she asked. "Do you want me to fix you something before you go? A sandwich?"

"No need," he assured her. "I already made one." He held up a bag with a grin.

She smiled. "I'll see you later, then."

Jedidiah waited patiently for him as Nate left the house, crossed the yard and climbed onto the wagon seat next to him. "*Gut* morning," Jed greeted.

"'Tis a *gut* day," Nate responded. "Where are we headed today?"

"New Holland."

He raised an eyebrow. "That's quite some distance away."

"We're meeting a crew near Whittier's Store where a driver and car will be waiting for us."

Nate was relieved. He didn't want to be gone longer than necessary. If he kept her too long from her family, Charlie might not return. For Jacob, he assured himself.

Jed steered his buggy toward the road. "Is that Charlie I just saw in the window?"

"*Ja*, she's staying with Jacob today." He explained about his brother's injury and Charlie's arrival on the scene of the accident. Jed expressed concern, then understanding as he explained how he wanted to keep news of Jacob's injuries quiet. Happiness was a small community. If word got out, everyone would know and natter about it. Then someone was liable to say something to upset his father when he called to check in.

Jed grinned.

Nate scowled. "Why are you grinning?"

"Charlie helping out with Jake. She's growing up."

He sighed. Yes, he'd noticed. "She's been a big help."

Jed agreed quietly and quickly changed the subject as he drove toward Whittier's Store.

Nate relaxed, glad that the topic of Charlie had been dropped as they headed toward a job that would earn him the remainder of what he needed to finalize the purchase of his farm.

Charlie hadn't wanted to come, but none of her sisters were available and she'd promised that someone would be here to stay with Jacob. She watched Nate and Jed leave then went into the great room to check on her patient. "Do you want anything?" she asked. "Coffee? Something to eat?"

He shook his head. "*Nay*, but how about a game of Dutch Blitz?"

"Are you sure you want to play when you know that I can beat you?"

Jacob chuckled. "I'll take my chances. This isn't baseball."

She snickered. "Where are the cards?"

"In the cabinet to the left of the kitchen sink."

The morning went quickly as Charlie showed Jake just how well she could play by beating him at three games. But by the time lunchtime arrived, however, they'd won a total of five games each.

Charlie chose to clean the house after lunch. She started upstairs, dusting, sweeping floors and collecting dirty laundry. She had cleaned the bathroom when she heard thumping steps in the hallway outside the room. She was shocked to see Jacob on the landing. "What are you doing up here?"

The embarrassed look on his face told her all she needed to know. "Call out if you need help with the stairs."

With laundry basket under her left arm, she descended the stairs then went to put the wash on. She returned to the great room to check on Jacob when she realized that he hadn't come downstairs yet. She resisted the urge to check on him, knowing that she'd further embarrass him if she did. Heading into the kitchen, she decided to plan supper. She had no idea what time Nate would be home, but she didn't want him to worry about fixing a meal.

She put on the ingredients for beef stew, then debated whether or not to make biscuits to go with it. Charlie heard several loud thumps and a masculine yelp. Heart thundering in her chest, she raced to the stairs to find that Jacob had fallen down the steps.

"Are you hurt?"

"*Nay*, I'm *oll recht*," Jacob said but when he tried to stand, he gasped, turned white and couldn't get up.

"I'm taking you to the doctor." Eyeing him with concern, Charlie calculated the time it would take for her to drive Jacob herself. "Don't move. I'm going to get help."

Jacob nodded. "Trust me. I won't. It hurts too much when I do."

Charlie shut off the stove before she left the house. She ran toward the road and down the street until she reached the closest *Eng-lisher*'s house. She knocked on the door and was relieved when a young woman answered. "I'm sorry to bother you, but may I use your phone? My friend hurt himself and I need to call Rick or Jeff Martin to take us to the doctor."

"I know Rick," the woman, who said her name was Molly, said. "Who needs medical attention?"

"Jacob Peachy."

She looked concerned. "I know the family. I'll call Rick and see if he or Jeff can come to the house. If not, I'll find someone who can. I'd take you myself but my baby is napping. If I can't find anyone else, I'll wake up my son."

Charlie smiled with relief. "Thank you. I should get back to the *haus*. I don't want to leave him alone for long."

"Someone will be by soon," the woman promised.

She raced back to the house. Jacob still hadn't moved and she was both glad, yet worried, that he'd listened to her. Charlie sat down beside him on the floor and waited for help to arrive. "Someone will be coming soon," she assured him. "I want to write Nate a note. Did he leave a phone number where he can be reached?" Her cousin's wife, Sarah, would have it, but she couldn't leave Jacob.

"It's in the right top kitchen drawer."

She found it just where Jacob had told her it would be. Charlie grabbed the paper to bring with her. She'd call Nate's construction boss, using a phone at the clinic. In the event the man couldn't get word to Nate, she wrote a quick note to explain what had happened.

What was taking so long? she wondered with concern. What if Jacob had pulled out his stitches under his foot brace? She felt responsible. She should have never left him alone upstairs.

A loud pounding on the door announced the help's arrival. Charlie answered the door, glad to recognize Jeff Martin. Within minutes Jeff had placed Jacob in the backseat of his car.

Jeff got them to the emergency room within minutes. She and Jeff waited while Jacob was wheeled into a back room.

"He'll be okay," Jeff said reassuringly.

"I hope so." She gazed at him with worry. "It was my fault that he fell."

"I doubt that," the man said.

Nate. She needed to call him. She stood. "I have to find a phone to call Nate."

Jeff nudged her arm to gain her attention and handed her his cell phone.

She smiled her thanks then dialed the number, relieved when Nate's construction boss answered. She explained the situation to Mike but then learned, to her dismay, that Nate had left the job for the day. "Nate already left work. May I make another call?"

"Feel free. You don't have to ask."

Charlie dialed her sister's cell phone number. She explained to Ellie what happened and asked if she could somehow get in touch with Nate.

"I'll get a hold of him," Ellie promised.

"Danki," Charlie said and hung up. She fought the urge to cry as she gave Jeff back his phone. She had to stay strong for Jacob—and for Nate.

Nate was tired when he got home. The day had been long and the work heavy but he didn't regret it. He'd made the money he needed.

He saw the buggy in the yard and smiled. Charlie would have fixed something for dinner. She was generous like that, and since Jacob's accident, he wondered how he could have managed without her.

Jed pulled in close to the house, and Nate

got out. "Let me know if Mike needs help again," he said.

"Will do." Jed eyed him with a half smile. "Say *hallo* to my cousin."

He didn't acknowledge his friend's teasing. "Will do."

After Jed left, Nate headed toward the house. The sound of buggy wheels caught his attention. He was surprised to see James Pierce, Charlie's brother-in-law, climb out of the vehicle seconds later.

"James," Nate greeted.

"Nate." James's somber expression caused Nate immediate concern.

"What's wrong?"

As James explained, Nate felt increasing alarm.

"Do you know which medical center they went to?"

"*Ja.* The emergency room at Lancaster General. Come with me and I'll take you to Drew." His friend Drew was the veterinarian who took over the practice after James left to join the Amish church and marry Charlie's sister Nell. James now took care of farm animals while Drew gave medical care for the animals brought into the clinic.

"Why are we going to see Drew?" Nate asked, confused.

"Drew's done for the day. He'll drive you to the hospital."

Nate understood. *"Danki."*

"Do you need anything inside the house?"

Nate started to shake his head then changed his mind. "I'll be just a minute." He entered the kitchen, saw a note lying on the table. Charlie had written it in a hurry but she'd let him know that they'd gone to the doctor after his brother's tumble down the stairs.

He saw a pot of beef stew on the stove and moved it into the refrigerator. Then, with pounding heart, he rushed to don clean garments before hurrying to rejoin James. Charlie's brother-in-law filled him in with what he'd learned as they headed toward the animal clinic. Drew was waiting for them when they arrived. Nate thanked James and Drew as he climbed into Drew's car. James promised to check in with him by phone later.

Charlie closed her eyes and leaned back in her chair in the waiting room. What was taking the doctor so long with news? How badly was Jacob hurt?

Her throat tightened. The day had begun well with Jake and her playing games. She should have put off cleaning house. Or stayed upstairs and waited for him. She could have helped him down the steps and prevented his fall. A tear leaked from her right eye to trail down her cheek. She sensed someone's presence above her and knew immediately that it was Nate. She opened her eyes.

Nate gazed down at her, his expression unreadable. "Charlie."

Wiping her eyes, she sprang to her feet as he stepped back. "The doctor hasn't come out to tell us anything." She saw that he'd changed out of his work clothes.

"What happened?" His voice was quiet as if prepared to hear the worst.

Charlie told in detail and looked away with a flush of guilt as she did. She felt the increasing tension in Nate, knew he blamed her as much as she blamed herself. She fought the strongest urge to leave. She needed to know how Jacob was and to face his brother's anger, which she deserved.

A man wearing a white lab coat exited from the treatment area and looked at her as he approached. She stood and gestured toward Nate, who had risen from his seat. "This is Nate Peachy. Jacob's brother."

The doctor nodded. "Despite the fall, your brother isn't as seriously hurt as he could have been. He tore open his stitches. I restitched him then put on a stronger and shorter cast.

He has a few bumps and bruises, but nothing that won't heal in a couple of weeks. I'd like to see him again in a few days to make sure everything is healing as well as it should."

"Do I bring him back here?" Nate asked, his features full of concern.

"I'm on call today. It'd be better if you came to my office." He handed Nate a business card. "Don't let him walk on his injured foot until after I check him again."

"I'll make sure he doesn't," Charlie said.

Nate shot her an even look that made her stomach burn. Clearly, he'd had enough of her help with Jacob. He was angry with her and no longer wanted her help.

An orderly pushed Jacob out of the back room minutes after a nurse went over Jake's discharge papers with them. His eyes widened when he saw his brother. "Nate."

"Are you *oll recht*?"

"*Ja*, I'll live. I'm sorry."

"You have no reason to be sorry." Nate's refusal to look at Charlie confirmed her worst fears.

Determined not to cry, she preceded the brothers out of the building where Jeff Martin waited to take them home. "All set?" Jeff asked.

"*Ja*," Charlie said quietly. She leaned close

to the kind *Englisher* and whispered, "Will you take me home first?"

Jeff studied her a long moment. "Of course." He shot a look at the brothers before returning his attention to her. "Would you like to ride up front?"

She managed a grateful smile. "I would," she whispered.

Chapter Five

Nate was silent as Jeff pulled his car into the Arlin Stoltzfus driveway.

"You're not coming home with us?" Jacob asked with disappointment.

Charlie gave him a small smile. "Nate will be with you. You don't need me."

"And I'll be home tomorrow, too," Nate said, drawing her glance. "We won't need you then, either."

Jacob frowned. "Don't you have to bale hay?"

"Not tomorrow."

"But I'll be fine with Charlie."

"I'm staying home," Nate said gruffly. "I'm sure Charlie has other things to do."

She hid her pain. "Thank you, Jeff. I don't know what we would've done without you."

"You're more than welcome, Charlie." The

man regarded her warmly. "Rest up. You look exhausted."

She spun toward the house without looking back at either brother in the rear seat. She'd reached the bottom of the front porch steps when the door opened and Ellie flew down the stairs.

"How's Jacob?" she asked after a quick glance toward the car.

"He's doing better," Charlie said, "but the doctor wants to see him back in a couple of days to make sure." She couldn't resist one last look at the vehicle as Jeff drove past toward the road. The action brought Nate's side of the car into view. His eyes seared hers briefly through the window before she averted her gaze. Her chest hurt. Her heart ached, and she felt perilously close to tears.

"*Mam* fixed supper. You hungry?"

Charlie shook her head. "I'm tired. Do you think she'll be upset if I go to bed?"

Worry settled on her sister's brow as Ellie studied her. "What's wrong?"

"I'm fine. Just tired. 'Tis been a long day."

"I'll tell *Mam* you're resting upstairs."

It was still early evening. Charlie could only imagine what her mother would think after Ellie told her that she'd gone to bed.

She pulled back the bed covering and slid

beneath the quilt with her clothes on. Her entire body ached, and her emotions were all over the place. She'd done the best she could under the circumstances, but it hadn't been good enough. She was the reason that Jacob had fallen, and it'd been clear that Nate blamed her.

After a good quiet cry, Charlie slipped into a restless sleep. It was dark outside when she woke and sensed a presence in her room. She wasn't afraid, for she knew instinctively that it was her mother. A flashlight clicked on, confirming her identity.

"*Mam,*" she murmured.

"Are you ill?"

"Just tired," she admitted. "And my head hurts."

Mam brushed light fingers over Charlie's forehead. "Ellie said that Jacob fell down the steps."

Charlie inhaled sharply. "*Ja,* he did."

"And you got him to a doctor."

She nodded.

"What happened?"

She told her about the events leading up to Jacob's tumble down the stairs.

"Tough day," *Mam* murmured.

"*Ja.*" She looked away, unwilling to let her

mam see how much Nate's reaction to Jake's accident had hurt her.

"What time will you be going tomorrow?"

Charlie shuddered out a sigh. "I'm not going to the Peachys'. I'll be here if you need anything. I can do the laundry."

Her mother was silent a long moment. "You're not going," she said with a frown.

"Nate asked me not to come." She sniffed. "He's staying home with Jacob."

Mam stood. "He probably thought you needed a rest after the day you had today… and you *were* tired." She caressed Charlie's cheek. "Sleep well, *dochter*."

She didn't really believe that was Nate's reason for telling her to stay home, but her mother's touch made her feel better. Charlie rolled over, closed her eyes and comforted by her *mam*'s love, she fell into a deep sleep.

The next morning she woke early and headed to the barn. She wanted to spend time with the animals, especially the horses. She loved horses. There was something calming about them.

Charlie fed the animals then put the cows and goats out to pasture. She then returned inside to brush the gelding her father had purchased recently. She found brushing Buddy's chestnut coat soothing. Immersed in the task, she didn't immediately detect a presence behind her.

"Charlie."

She spun, gasped. "Nathaniel! What are you doing here?"

"I need to speak with you." Dressed in a blue shirt and navy tri-blend pants with black suspenders, he looked good. Too good.

She sighed, trying not to notice his appearance and the way her heart leaped. Flushing with guilt, she went back to brushing Buddy. "I know what you came to say, and I'm sorry."

His tension radiated from behind her. "About what?"

Charlie faced him with brush in hand. "It was my fault Jacob got hurt."

He frowned. "Did you push him down the stairs?"

"Nay!" She blinked as she registered his surprised expression. "I should have stayed upstairs and waited to help him down."

"He wouldn't have allowed it."

She eyed him curiously. "Then why did you tell me to stay home?"

She watched with astonishment as Nate's features softened. "You were exhausted. I was worried about you. It was a bad day yesterday and I thought you might need some time to yourself."

Charlie studied him a long moment. "Maybe I do," she said, thinking of her plans to visit Bishop John. "Then why are you here?"

"To thank you and to ask for your help. I heard from my *dat*. My *grossmudder* is ill, and my family will be staying in Indiana for another week."

"You need someone to stay with Jacob."

Nate stared at her. "*Ja*. You."

"I don't know if that's a *gut* idea."

He nodded. "I understand."

"Why me?" she dared.

"Because you have done a great job with Jacob and with the *haus*."

She felt both pleased and annoyed. She'd rather hear that he missed her than he missed her cooking and cleaning...and brother-sitting services, but she supposed the fact that he trusted her enough to want her back meant something.

"Well?" he asked.

"Well what?"

He studied her with patience. "Will you come back tomorrow?"

"I don't think so," she admitted. She had a terrible night, thanks to Nathaniel Peachy. She wasn't going to rush and jump in to help out, even though she wanted nothing more than to do so. "But I know for a fact that Ellie will be available to come tomorrow." She bit her lip. "How is Jake?"

"He's in pain, but the medicine helps."

"I'm sorry." She blinked rapidly and looked away. Resuming the task at hand, she kept her gaze focused on the horse.

Suddenly, Nate stood next to her. Close. Too close. He reached up to still her hand with his warm fingers. "I hope you'll be the one to stay with Jacob...if you're free." Then he turned and left her. She sighed and wondered how she was going to stay away from the Peachy farm. It would be hard now that Nate had asked nicely for her return.

Charlie hugged herself with her arms. She shouldn't, but she cared for him a great deal. He'd called her a child. He regarded her as a girl helpful but troublesome. There was nothing she could do to make him see her differently, she realized with sadness. Nothing to convince him that she was a responsible young woman...who was falling in love with him.

Nate had risen early, taken care of the animals then returned to the house to make breakfast. Today he would spend the day with Jacob. He had to bale hay soon, but not yet. He'd been shaken by the news that Jacob had fallen down the steps. After they'd returned home, he'd debated whether or not he should call his parents. He changed his mind after receiving word late last night that his grandmother had become ill and his family would be gone another week. He didn't want to further worry his father. Jacob would recover, while he had no idea how bad his *grossmudder*'s condition was.

He'd lain awake last night, obsessing over Charlie. She'd looked crestfallen yesterday when he'd told her to stay home. It had occurred to him during the night that she might have misunderstood the reason. It wasn't that he didn't trust her with Jacob's well-being. On the contrary, she'd done a good job getting Jacob medical attention. No, his concern was for her. She'd given them so much of her time, and he figured she was ready for a break. Which was why he'd gone to see her first thing this morning to explain, in case she'd had the wrong idea. And she had.

After his return from the Stoltzfus residence, Nate parked his buggy in the barnyard and hurried inside the house to check on his brother. He was relieved to find Jacob asleep. He wrote him a note to stay put—just in case—before he headed out to the barn to let the horses, goats and cows into the pasture.

He watched the horses run in the fields and thought again of Charlie. If only she was older. If only she wasn't like Emma, then maybe…

The best thing for the both of them would be if Charlie sent one of her sisters to stay with Jacob.

He needed coffee. He returned to the house and put on a fresh pot then searched through the pantry for something to eat. *Charlie has been busy,* he thought with a pang as he spied a plate of muffins, a fresh loaf of bread and a pie plate with the remains of an apple pie. He pulled out the bread and then grabbed butter from the refrigerator.

The coffee finished perking, and he poured himself a cup and added a spoon of sugar with a splash of cream. He brought it to the table, then grabbed a piece of bread and buttered it. His hand stilled in midaction as something occurred to him. The church elders would be seeking a permanent teacher for their Happiness School. Elizabeth Troyer would be leaving soon. Which left the opening for Charlie.

Nate grinned as he picked up his coffee. "She can start next week," he murmured before he took a sip. His grin faded. It would be a wonderful opportunity for Charlie, but it would also mean that she wouldn't ever be back to help with Jacob. He exhaled sharply. He didn't know how he felt about that.

After Charlie's sister came tomorrow, Nate would head out to speak with the bishop about Charlie.

He was shocked to realize that he'd miss her. Given his past with Emma, he shouldn't feel this way, but somehow Charlie had gotten deeply under his skin.

Because she's good with Jacob, he reasoned. He'd miss her help, her cooking…and her smile. *Because of Jacob.* Something inside him suggested differently, but he buried the feeling.

"I appreciate you staying with Jake today, Ellie," Charlie said.

"I'm available. I don't mind." Ellie studied her thoughtfully. "What are you going to do?"

"I plan to talk with Bishop John about the *schuul*teacher position."

Surprise flickered across Ellie's expression. "You want to teach *schuul*?"

Charlie frowned. "I thought you knew that. I'm sure I told you."

Her sister shook her head. "*Nay.* I would have remembered if you had." Ellie smiled. "*Gut* for you."

"I hope I get a chance to teach," she said, giving voice to her fears.

"Why do you say that? You'd be a great teacher."

She softened her expression and she smiled. "*Danki*, Ellie. I hope the church elders agree."

"What am I supposed to do once I get to the Peachys'?"

"Keep Jacob company, fix him and maybe Nate lunch. I made a grocery list for Nate, but I don't know if he's had a chance to shop. You can always call Nell and ask her to bring you a few things."

Her sisters Ellie and Nell were the only two in the family with cell phones, allowed by the church elders because of their lines of work with Nell as part of her husband's veterinary practice, and Ellie because she cleaned houses for a living.

"Don't worry, I'll take *gut* care of him."

It wasn't Jacob she was worried about. It was Nate. She smiled her thanks. Charlie brushed a hand down the length of her white apron that she tied over her purple tab dress. "How do I look?"

Ellie smiled. "Vanity, *schweschter*? I'm shocked."

"I'm not vain… I don't think." At least she hoped not since vanity was a sin. "I need a little confidence for when I meet with Bishop John. It won't be easy to convince him that I'm the best person to be teacher."

She accompanied Ellie until she reached her vehicle. She climbed into the family market wagon while her sister got into her pony cart. She then waved at Ellie before she drove in the opposite direction.

As she parked the wagon close to Bishop John Fisher's house, Charlie felt a wild nervous fluttering in her chest. She sat unmoving in the wagon for several minutes. Too much hinged on this meeting, she thought.

Would the bishop remind her of every misdeed of her youth? Would he tell her that she was out of luck since the elders had already found a replacement?

She drew a calming breath then climbed down from her vehicle, went to the side entrance and rapped on the wooden door. Within seconds the door opened, revealing Sally Hershberger Fisher, who looked surprised but delighted to see her.

"Charlie!" the woman welcomed with a smile. "Come in!"

"*Hallo*, Sally. 'Tis nice to see you." She glanced down at Sally's pregnant belly and flashed her a genuine smile of pleasure. "How are you feeling?"

Sally smiled. "I'm well." She stepped aside and gestured Charlie into the kitchen. "Wonderful, actually. I'm feeling great and…" Her hands cradling her stomach, she leaned close and whispered, "I'm so happy."

Charlie beamed at her. "I'm pleased for you."

"Danki." Sally eyed her intently. "Would you like tea or coffee?"

She shook her head. "I need to talk with Bishop John. Is he available?"

"Ja. Let me tell him that you're here." Looking curious, but clearly unwilling to pry, Sally studied her for a long moment before she left the room. She was back within seconds. "He's happy to see you. Come with me."

Charlie started to follow then froze as her chest tightened and she suddenly found it difficult to breathe. As if sensing Charlie's hesitation, Sally stopped and faced her. She must have read something in Charlie's expression because she quickly returned to her side. "Is everything *oll recht*?"

"I…" Why was she so nervous? If she didn't get the job, what would it matter? *It would matter to me*, she realized. It was important and she wanted her chance. "Sally, I've come to talk with John about the teaching position. Do I even have a chance? I know I was impulsive and a bit reckless when I was younger, but I'm not the same person now," she said, hugging herself with her arms.

Sally's expression softened. "I think you'd be a wonderful teacher."

She blinked. "You do?"

The bishop's wife nodded. "Go in and talk with him. Let him know you're interested. The decision isn't John's alone. He may not be able to give you an answer right away, but you won't be considered if no one knows how much you want to teach."

Closing her eyes, Charlie exhaled sharply. "I do want to teach." She bit her lip. "A lot."

"Then tell him that," Sally urged as she led Charlie down the hall until they reached the room where John handled church district business.

"John, Charlie's here," Sally announced then left the two of them alone.

Charlie stood a moment, wondering how to start.

"Have a seat, Charlotte."

Her heart hammered as she nodded and sat down.

Chapter Six

Charlie wore her spring-green dress. Matt Troyer, her sister's brother-in-law, had told her once that the dress brightened the color of her eyes. It wasn't vanity that drove her to wear it, she assured herself. It was just that she needed the confidence in knowing that she looked her best when she saw Nate again. The man made her nervous, and her heart fluttered whenever he was near.

She brought a lemon pound cake that she'd baked especially for the brothers last evening. She got out of the vehicle then reached onto the seat to retrieve it. She straightened and started toward the Abram Peachy house only to realize that the door to the farmhouse was open. Nate Peachy stood on the threshold, watching her approach.

Charlie didn't smile as she walked toward

the house. There was no warmth in Nate's expression and the tension between them was thick. She felt it in her tight throat and the painful butterflies that fluttered in her belly. "Nate," she greeted just before he stepped aside to allow her entry.

His lack of reply halted her in her tracks and made her face him. She arched an eyebrow.

"You came back," he said.

"Looks like it," she replied briskly. Was he unhappy that Ellie hadn't returned?

A sudden smile hovered on his lips, making him even more attractive to her. She tried not to feel flustered. "Where's Jake?"

His good humor disappeared. "In the other room." She started toward the great room and he grabbed her arm to stop her. "I made an arrangement so that there will be no need for him to go upstairs..."

She blushed. "I understand. That's *gut. Ja, gut*."

Nate's gaze warmed. Shaken by his look, Charlie spun and headed in to see his brother.

Jacob was seated on the upholstered chair with his leg propped up.

He looked up at her with a smile when she approached him. She responded in kind, her mouth curving with happiness to see him looking much better and not in pain.

"Charlie! You're here!"

She grinned. "How else will I be able to trounce you in cards again?"

Jacob chuckled. His features changed as he glanced past her shoulder to his brother. "You baling hay today?"

Nate nodded. "Not to worry, though. It'll get done. I've got the Lapp *bruders* coming to help out."

She eyed him with horror. "My cousins are coming?" When he nodded, she exclaimed, "But what will I fix? There will be many mouths to feed!"

Jacob scowled. "Hey! Who will keep me company?"

"I will. Only we'll be in the kitchen instead of out here." Charlie looked at Nate. "What are you still doing here? Don't you have work to do?" She gasped, as if realizing just what she'd said.

Nate's astonishment quickly turned to amusement. "*Ja*, Charlie." He spun to leave.

"Wait!" she called. "Can you help me get Jacob into the kitchen so he won't have to sit out here alone?"

Nate stared at her a moment before he nodded. He left the room and headed toward the stairs but then returned moments later with a wheelchair. "This should help," he said.

"Danki," she murmured and then watched Nate help his brother into the chair.

When she reached for it, Nate waved her away. "I'll push him."

Didn't he trust her to push Jake into the other room? She hoped that wasn't the case, but she couldn't help feeling that it was.

As Nate moved Jacob into the kitchen, Charlie heard vehicles in the barnyard. She went to the window and was pleased to see five of her Lapp male cousins. Upon seeing her through the glass, Jed waved. She saw him murmur something to his brothers and suddenly all five turned to stare at her. Blushing, she pulled back, eager to get to work. First thing she'd do was make coffee. Then she'd think about what food to prepare for lunch. She'd have to decide what to fix for supper, but she had a feeling that by the end of the day her cousins would want to go home to eat with their wives.

Without thought, Charlie poured Jacob coffee, fixed it the way he liked it and set a bowl of cereal before him. Jacob looked at the coffee and his breakfast, then grinned. She realized that she hadn't asked what he wanted, but he was pleased. She smiled back, knowing instinctively that she'd given him exactly what he wanted. She'd learned a lot about Jacob in the past few days and found that she liked the young man a lot. Despite his injuries, he still managed to smile and show gratitude for whatever she did for him.

Charlie thought of Nate and turned away from the table. No need for Jacob to know that she'd had serious doubts about returning today because of his brother. And her feelings for Nate.

Her cousins had peeked in to say a quick hello. After they went outside, Charlie handed Nate a pair of gloves. "Don't need you getting hurt like your brother."

He looked startled by her concern but took the gloves before he left to join her cousins in the hayfields. It was quiet with the men gone and Jacob silently reading a book. Charlie stared about the kitchen, wondering what to make for lunch. She needed to go grocery shopping—something she could handle tomorrow—but that wouldn't help her decide what to cook now. Feeding three was no problem, but having to make a meal for eight? That was something else altogether. She tensed as she started toward the refrigerator and opened the door wide.

Jacob looked up from his book. "What's upsetting you?" he asked, watching her closely.

"I don't know what to make for lunch."

He smiled. "Charlie, this is my *bruder* and your cousins. Cake, pie and cookies would be enough."

She gasped. "For dessert maybe, but not for lunch." She shut the refrigerator door. "I'm going to check the freezer." She started toward the back room, worried that she couldn't pull off a meal to be proud of, even though lunch was still a few hours from now. Charlie gasped when Jacob grabbed her arm. He had risen from his chair to reach her. "Jacob! Be careful. I don't want you to fall and hurt yourself again."

"I'm fine. Steady as a rock. See? I'm holding on."

"What do you need?" She swallowed hard. If she caused Jacob to get hurt again—and if she messed up the meal, then she'd never live it down. And she'd feel terrible forever. And Nate would never forgive her.

"I need you to stop worrying," Jacob said. "You're amazing. You'll do fine."

She released a sharp breath. *"Danki."* She briefly closed her eyes. "I hope you're right."

"I'm always right," he said teasingly, which made her smile. He released her arm and lowered himself carefully into his chair. "Go look in the freezer, but I'm telling you desserts will be fine. If you want more, you can offer peanut butter and jam sandwiches. Nate and I love them."

She felt herself relax. "I'll see what I can do." She paused on the threshold between the kitchen and the back room. "What kind of cake?"

"Chocolate?"

She grinned. "I'll see if you have all the ingredients."

Jacob went back to his reading while she assembled what she considered a makeshift meal. She only hoped it would be enough food for five hungry farmworkers.

By the time the men returned to the house for lunch, Charlie had soup simmering on the stove and a plate of peanut butter with jam sandwiches on the kitchen counter ready to be served. She'd found three types of jam in the refrigerator—strawberry, peach and boysenberry. The soup was a simple chicken noodle recipe that her mother had taught her to make. There had been just enough frozen leftover cooked chicken. The bread was homemade, and she'd made chocolate cake with fudge frosting that morning. And there was the lemon cake she'd brought with her.

She stood, watching as the men filed in. Her cousin Noah grinned at her when he saw the chocolate cake. Everyone in the family knew Noah's preference for anything chocolate. She had no idea what Nate liked best, but she hoped he'd be satisfied with the meal she'd provided.

"Smells *gut* in here," her cousin Jedidiah said.

"Chicken soup?" his brother Isaac declared as he moved to look in the pot on the stove. He grinned as he faced the others. "*Ja*, chicken soup with lots of noodles!"

Her fraternal twin cousins, Jacob and Elijah, expressed their appreciation as they took a seat at the table. Since all of their hands were clean, Charlie knew the men must have washed up outside despite the cold weather.

She chanced a look toward Nate, who chatted with Jed as he took his seat at the long trestle table. Worried whether or not she'd done well in the kitchen, she filled soup dishes from the pot on the stove, then carefully set a bowl before each man. Then she grabbed the dish of sandwiches from the counter and set them in the middle of the table. She'd placed small plates at each setting earlier.

"Peanut butter and jam sandwiches?" Elijah asked.

Tensing, Charlie nodded.

Her cousin beamed at her. "Yum."

She smiled and turned for the pitcher of iced tea. As she spun back, she caught Nate watching her with an odd expression. Feeling her face heat, she looked away, unwilling to let him know how much he affected her.

The men ate their soup and sandwiches while they discussed the work they'd accomplished. She gleaned from their conversation that the hay was pushed into rows, which would be swept up from the field later by the baler. She knew what the work entailed, although she'd never been allowed to bale hay. A worker would run the baler over the rows of cut hay then bales would come out the end and be placed onto a platform. Once the platform on the baler was full, the bales of hay would be moved into wagons that would transport them closer to the barn. When they were done baling, the men would move the hay bales into a storage building on the property.

Charlie didn't eat or sit. She stood at the counter, listening. Not wanting to appear nosy, she worked to put away the dishes she used and washed earlier. She felt out of sorts, as if she didn't belong, despite the fact that Nate had asked her to come and the others were her cousins.

"I'll oversee the baler," Nate said.

"Nay," Jed protested. "You already have one Peachy man down. We'll not be taking a chance that you'll get hurt, too." He paused. "You can steer it."

"You all have wives and children. I don't," Nate insisted.

"I can do it," Isaac said. "I have a wife but no children."

Charlie snorted. "Yet," she said with a snicker. The women of the family had recently learned that Isaac's wife, Ellen, was with child.

Isaac smiled sheepishly at his brothers, and Nate raised his eyebrows as he offered his congratulations.

"That's it, then. I'll work behind the baler."

"Nate, it takes more than one man to run the machine. We'll take turns."

Nate gazed at his friends. "Fine. We'll take turns, then, and be very careful."

The men stood after finishing their lunch that ended with the chocolate and lemon cakes for dessert. Charlie was pleased that no one turned a slice down. Jacob asked for a second piece. Noah enjoyed a huge piece and asked Charlie if another one could be packed up for him to take. She laughed and told him she'd have it ready and waiting for him.

"Great meal, Charlie," Jed said.

Her other cousins echoed his sentiment. Nate hadn't said anything as he stood.

"Nate," Jacob said, "would you mind helping me into the other room?"

"I'm sorry, Jake," Charlie said. "I should have realized you'd had enough of the kitchen."

"I enjoyed watching you work," he assured her as Nate brought the wheelchair close and helped his brother into it.

Charlie started to collect the dishes and stack them on the counter near the sink while Nate pushed Jacob into the other room. She ran water into the dish basin and added a squirt of dish soap, then turned off the spigot when the basin was full. She grabbed a sandwich plate and was washing it when Nate reentered the kitchen. He didn't say anything, and her discomfort grew. She was afraid that he wasn't happy with what she'd made for lunch—or that she'd kept Jacob in the kitchen for too long.

She tried to ignore him and the lump in her throat as she continued to wash dishes before setting them in the drain rack. Sensing that Nate hadn't moved, she spun to face him.

"*What?* Is there something you want to say?" She blinked rapidly as she eyed him defiantly. He studied her a moment before he nodded slowly. "I know it wasn't the best meal, but I used what I had available," she muttered.

He frowned as she glared at him. "It was a *gut* meal," he said quietly. But his expression didn't clear.

She scowled as she wondered whether she'd done something wrong.

Nate started to approach then halted. "Don't look at me that way. I was just thinking that you made an amazing meal with little in the cupboard. I should have bought groceries," he said huskily. "I'm sorry."

Charlie felt a jolt. He was apologizing? That was the last thing she'd expected from him. "You didn't mind peanut butter and jam sandwiches?"

His features smoothed out as he gave her a genuine smile. "I love peanut butter and jam sandwiches." A look of amusement entered his blue eyes. "I'm sure Jacob gave away that little secret."

She felt her lips curve in response. "He might have mentioned it, but I wasn't sure if sandwiches were enough for you. You've all been working hard."

"You also made us chicken noodle soup and

cakes." He chuckled. "I've never seen anyone enjoy chocolate cake more than Noah."

She grinned. "'Tis common knowledge in our family that he loves chocolate."

He gazed at her with tenderness for several seconds. "I need to get back to work."

His expression serious again, he headed toward the door.

"Be careful," she called.

He halted and faced her. There was something in his eyes she couldn't read, but it was a look that somehow terrified and excited her. "I will," he murmured before he left.

Charlie went to the window and watched through an opening in the sheer white curtains as Nate joined her cousins in the yard. She saw him laugh at something Elijah said. The sight of his grin and happy face made her reel with pleasure. She cared for Nate Peachy. Too much. Maybe it would be best if she asked one of her sisters to stay with Jacob tomorrow, provided that Jacob still needed someone to come.

After she'd fixed herself a sandwich, put away the leftover food and cleaned the kitchen, Charlie went to check on Jacob. She smiled when she saw him seated in the wheelchair by the window. His foot was propped up on the ever-present wooden chair and he was fast asleep. Jacob was a good man. *And so is his* bruder. Her heart thumped hard as she returned to the kitchen. She shouldn't be thinking about Nate. She was here for Jacob and she had to remember that.

She grabbed pencil and paper from the kitchen drawer then sat at the table to make a grocery list. Nate and Jacob would need to shop for food now that their family wouldn't be home for another week.

There was no telling if Nate would want her to come again after he finished making hay. He'd be around for Jacob then and he'd no longer need her. Still, they would need food. She checked the refrigerator for basic items, then she wrote the low or missing items on the list. There wasn't much flour left, she thought. The least she could do before she left was to make a few loaves of bread for them to eat after she was gone. She closed her eyes as a wave of feeling washed over her. She'd miss Jacob. She'd miss Nate.

She rose from the chair and went to the kitchen window that overlooked the pasture and the farm fields beyond. She could make out the men working some distance away, knew that with her cousins' help, the hay-making would be completed sometime today. Charlie felt a little pang in her chest as she resumed her seat and forced herself to concentrate on what needed to be purchased. Laundry soap, she thought and wrote it down. "Vanilla and cocoa powder." One couldn't make a chocolate cake or brownies without them.

She lifted a hand to tuck a tiny strand of red hair under her prayer *kapp* as she tried to think what else they needed. It had been a busy morning and she felt less put together. Charlie reached up and removed her *kapp* and combed fingers over her hair before donning her head covering. List complete for now, she stood and walked around the kitchen suddenly feeling at a loss. She felt antsy. She needed to do something. She'd visit the horses in the barn but she didn't want to leave Jacob alone in case he needed her. If he was awake, she could tell him where she was going and be confident that he would stay put until her return.

"You *oll recht* up there?" Jed asked.

Nate flashed him an amused glance. "I'm fine. What's the matter? Getting tired of walking along beside the baler, Jed?"

"He can always trade places with me," Isaac said from where he steered the equipment.

"I'm fine," Isaac's older brother said with a scowl.

Laughing, Nate said, "Don't look fine to me." He looked across the property to where the other Lapp brothers were working another hay baler. "You can always switch with Elijah," he suggested, noting that Elijah was positioned on the baler like he was.

"You don't look fine, Nate," Isaac said. "You keep looking toward the *haus*. Something or someone there on your mind?"

"Jacob?"

"I was thinking that maybe you've been thinking about my cousin."

Nate froze. "Not likely. Jacob is the one who's hurt. Charlie is just here to help."

"I'm surprised you didn't ask Mae to come by."

Mae King was Nate's stepgrandmother. "The less people who know the better," Nate said. "Charlie was there when Jake had his accident. We worked out an arrangement for her to stay with him while I was working."

"And that's all?"

Nate's throat tightened. "*Ja*, that's all. What else would it be?"

Isaac flashed him a crafty look. "*Ja*, what else can it be?"

He noticed one of the Lapp twins, Jacob,

driving the wagon of baled hay in their direction. "Wagon's full," Nate called, eager to end the conversation about Charlie. Did they see something in his expression that gave his thoughts away? He only wanted to help Charlie. There was nothing more to his friendship with her. Distracted, he started to climb down from the baler and slipped.

"You *oll recht*?" Isaac asked.

"Fine." But his heart beat rapidly as he recalled how easily someone could get hurt after a fall. His thoughts went again to Charlie. She'd been on his mind too often lately. But he got a chill as he envisioned her on the mower, the danger in which she'd placed herself. He scowled. Why couldn't he get her out of his thoughts? She wasn't his responsibility. After the way he'd failed Emma, he was the least one capable enough to help her.

"'Tis nice to see Charlie mothering Jacob," Isaac said, bringing up his cousin again.

Jed continued to walk beside the baler. "Apparently, she has some nurturing instincts."

Despite himself, Nate couldn't control a smile as he held up his gloved hands. "She made me wear these." He snorted. "To protect my hands."

Isaac laughed. "'Tis funny that she'd be

thinking of safety when she is the one who frequently got hurt and into trouble."

"I haven't seen that side of her in a long time," he admitted.

"*Nay*, she's grown up." Isaac climbed down to walk alongside the baler while Nate got up into the seat behind the horses and Jed hopped up to exchange places with his brother Elijah near the back of the machine.

"*Ja*, she is." Elijah stepped onto the wagon attached to Nate's hay baler, catching the block of hay as it came out. "Charlie will make someone a *gut* wife one day. Matt Troyer seems interested."

Nate's jaw tightened. "I didn't know they were friends."

"His brother is Nell's husband," Isaac pointed out. The baler started to move and Isaac followed alongside on foot. "Her birthday is soon. *Mam* will be hosting a surprise nineteenth birthday party for her the day before. You, Jacob and your family should come if Jake is feeling up to it." He mentioned a date.

"My family should be home by then. I'll talk with Jacob and let you know."

"No need," Isaac said. "There'll be plenty of food. Just come if you can, and be *willkomm*."

Nate clicked his tongue as he flicked the

leathers to get his team of horses moving. As he drove, he found his mind wandering again to Charlie. *Nineteen years old. Not a girl, but a young woman.* He'd known it, of course, but somehow it seemed better for him to forget the age difference. Safer to think of her as a girl and not a woman. He tensed up at the memory of Isaac's teasing remarks. Yet, the image of her married to Matt with children of her own formed a knot in his belly. He forced it away, reminding himself of all the reasons that he shouldn't see Charlie as more than a girl…more than a friend.

Go to a surprise party for her? Why not? As long as Jacob was well enough. If not, they would stay home. It wasn't as if Charlie expected him to come. She didn't know about the party. If he attended, he could watch how she interacted with Matthew Troyer, to make sure he was someone who could make her happy…who could love and handle her, keeping her safe—and alive. The knot in his stomach intensified.

What could he give her for her birthday? He had a little time to think of something but still, he couldn't stop wondering about a gift.

The men grew silent as they worked. Nate was thoughtful as he drove down one row of cut hay then carefully maneuvered the baler onto the next row. What could he give Charlie that she would like? He recalled how she loved horses and the way she looked when he'd found her in the barn brushing the coat of a chestnut gelding.

A slow smile came to his lips as he had a germ of an idea. He could do it. He could make her something special that he was sure she'd enjoy.

"Christmas is almost here," Isaac commented. "I have no idea what to give everyone this year."

Elijah smirked. "You always give the right thing, *bruder.*"

"What about you, Nate? Do you think you'll have another little *bruder* or sister by Christmas?"

Nate shook his head. "Not supposed to. Baby is due in January." Men usually didn't talk about women's business, but he didn't mind. The Lapp brothers were his friends, and they were willing to discuss most any topic.

Jedidiah chuckled. "Babies don't always come when they're supposed to."

"'Tis going to snow soon," Isaac mentioned, changing the subject.

"You don't want to talk about babies," Jed said with a chuckle.

"Not supposed to," Isaac grumbled.

"I hope it doesn't snow," Nate said, understanding that a new father-to-be might be nervous. "At least, not until my family's safely home again."

"We usually have snow before Christmas," Jed pointed out, and the others agreed.

Isaac grabbed a hay bale and tossed it behind him onto the flatbed of the wagon. "Perhaps we should think about cutting pine and holly before it does."

"Won't last if we cut too early," Jed said.

Conversation lagged after a while as they stayed busy to complete the work.

Two hours later the men finished making hay. The bales were carted to an area outside the storage barn where they were wrapped in plastic to protect them from the elements of the weather. Tomorrow morning he'd move the rest of them into the building on his own. Jed and Noah had already moved most of the bales inside, so the work should be easy.

"I appreciate your help today," he told his friends. "The job was done in half the time because of you."

"We didn't mind. 'Tis only one day," Jed said. He glanced toward the sky and noted the setting sun. "But I do need to get going. Sarah will have supper ready."

"Martha will, too," Elijah murmured.

The other brothers made the same comment about their wives.

The men walked toward the barnyard where their vehicles were parked. "I'll come for the baler within the next couple of days," Jed said.

Nate nodded. "I'll be happy to bring it."

Jedidiah shook his head. "*Nay*, you've enough to worry about."

Minutes later the Lapp brothers left, and Nate headed toward the house. He wondered what Charlie was doing.

He pushed open the back door. No one was in the kitchen. *"Hallo?"* he called as he headed toward the great room. He entered to find Charlie and Jacob sitting close with only a small table between them. On the table surface sat a wooden board with six sides and slots with marbles. They hadn't heard him, as they were teasing each other while they played Aggravation. Hearing their shared laughter, Nate felt a kick to his gut. She was never that relaxed and carefree with him. But then, she and Jacob were close in age and it was only natural that they should like each other.

"Who's winning?" he asked loudly as he approached.

Charlie gasped and Jacob looked up with laughter. "I am," his brother said with a smug smile.

She returned her attention to Jacob. "Maybe this game, but I won the last five."

"Huh," Jacob muttered, and Nate chuckled, knowing that Charlie had spoken the truth.

He approached and stood over them. Charlie refused to meet his gaze, but he caught sight of a pulse fluttering at the base of her throat and wondered what she was thinking. "We're done making hay," he said.

She glanced up. "That's *gut*."

His lips twitched. "I wore the gloves you gave me all afternoon." He remember how she'd had handed them to him this morning right before he'd left for the fields.

"You listen well." His reward was her crooked smile. "Sometimes," she teased.

"What's wrong with your hands?" Jacob asked.

"Not a thing, and apparently Charlie wanted to make sure they stay that way." Nate pulled up a chair and studied the board. He felt her tense up as he leaned closer. "You going to let Jake win?" he asked, focusing on her flushed face.

Jacob grinned. "*Ja*, she is."

Charlie suddenly stood. "I'm sorry. 'Tis

late. I need to get home." She turned away and headed toward the kitchen.

"You intimidate her," Jacob said sharply.

He frowned. "*Nay*, I don't."

His brother bobbed his head. "*Ja*, you do."

"I don't mean to." Nate stood and left the room to go after her. He had many mixed feelings when it came to Charlie Stoltzfus, but the last thing he wanted to do was to scare her. When he entered the kitchen, she was putting away the last of the dishes.

"Charlie," he said gently.

She turned. "There is chicken corn chowder in the refrigerator," she replied briskly. "There should be enough for two meals. Tomorrow for breakfast, there are eggs and you can eat the biscuits I made today."

He watched her shift nervously about the room. "Charlie," he said softly, approaching to gently clasp her arm. "Tell me what's upsetting you."

She blinked as she jerked away. "Nothing. Why?"

Nate blew out a startled breath. "Are you afraid of me?"

"*Nay*," she said firmly. She eyed him with a level gaze that convinced him to believe her. His relief made him realize how happy he was that Jacob was wrong.

"Here's a grocery list." She handed it to him. "Just a few things that you could use." Her lips firmed. "You may want to consider buying meals that are easy to prepare." She bit her lip. "For when I'm not here."

He stiffened with his disappointment. "You're not coming tomorrow?"

Charlie wouldn't meet his gaze. "I have a few things to do."

"Christmas shopping?"

She shook her head. *"Nay."*

"I see." He knit his brow. "Will someone be here for Jacob?"

Her eyes briefly locked with his. "Probably Ellie again."

"I apologize if we've monopolized your time," he said gruffly.

She blinked. "You haven't. I came here to help because I wanted to."

He regarded her with tenderness. *"Danki."* He sharpened his gaze when she blushed and suddenly busied herself. She bustled about the room as if she needed to get all her work done. As if she didn't plan to return. He reached out to stop her frantic movement, his fingers surrounding her upper arm, turning her to face him. "Charlie. What is it? Why do I make you uncomfortable?"

Her green eyes bright, she shook her head.

"You don't." Her smile lacked luster, and he was upset because she had to work hard to convince herself that it wasn't true. "I should get home."

He had made her uneasy. He nodded. "May I carry something for you?"

"*Nay*, I've only this plate," she said, referring to the dish she'd brought with the lemon pound cake.

He followed her outside and waited as she climbed into her pony cart. "I appreciate everything you've done for us," he told her, watching her closely.

"I would have done the same for anyone," she said quickly. Then with a flick of the reins, she left while Nate stood in the yard, staring after her, wondering why it bothered him so much that she'd gone.

Chapter Seven

The weather was usual for mid-November. The air was crisp and clean with a hint of the upcoming winter. The leaves that had changed to reds, oranges and golds were now gone. The evergreens were full and thick and ready for the upcoming Christmas season. Soon the holiday would be here with the bitter-cold temperatures.

Nate headed out to haul the hay bales inside. As he carried one in, he couldn't keep his thoughts from Charlie. She hadn't come to the house this morning. Ellie had come in her place, after Charlie had claimed she had something to do. Had she been telling the truth? Or had he overwhelmed her with his desire to make sure she stayed safe?

There was something about the young red-haired woman that tugged on his heartstrings.

He couldn't get rid of the image of her lovely bright green eyes and pretty smile. She kept him on his toes. She had the ability to make those around her feel alive. Make him feel alive.

He stilled, his chest tight. It was wrong to think about her this way. He needed to keep his goals in mind, to get on with his life, settle on the farm property he wanted to purchase and find a suitable wife. Someone he couldn't fail, a more mature woman ready to start a family with a new husband. A woman unlike Emma...*or Charlie.*

As he moved bales into the building, he thought about the surprise party in less than two weeks. His whole family was invited. Going to the party would be a good way to show their appreciation for everything Charlie had done for them. He'd attend, then step back, put distance between them. He needed to find a way to cease worrying, obsessing, about her. How else could he move on to marry and have a family?

The air no longer felt chilly as he perspired while he worked. As he came out of the storage structure for the umpteenth time, he decided there had to be an easier way to move the rest of the hay. The stack hadn't looked big before he'd started, but its appearance had been deceiving.

Nate went into the barn to look for something to make the job easier. Then he saw the wooden wagon that he and his siblings had used when they were children, the wagon his younger half-siblings now enjoyed. It was larger than an English red wagon; his father had made it for five young children to share.

Nate pulled the wagon outside and began to load it with hay bales from the stack. He was able to tote four bales in the wagon. In a short time he'd completed the work, satisfied that the hay would stay dry. As he put away the wagon, he debated whether or not he should grocery-shop. There was enough food for lunch, he decided. He could put off shopping until the afternoon.

While in the barn, he spied a pile of wood scraps in the back corner of an empty stall. He rummaged through the pile and found a block of wood that had been left over from a previous construction project. He examined the piece from all angles and decided it was just what he needed. It was perfect for carving into. Nate smiled. The smooth, hard surface would be the basis for what he had in mind for Charlie's birthday present. He retrieved his pocketknife and two pieces of sandpaper from a worktable then headed toward a bright corner of the barn where he sat down to work.

As the wood fell away in shavings, Nate grinned. The scent of wood and straw was thick in the air. He had a vision to create, and he found pleasure in the work as he brought it to life.

Would Charlie like his present? Why should he care whether or not she did? He had a feeling that she would, but he couldn't be certain.

Nate sighed as he continued to work his knife. Why did his every thought return to Charlie?

He focused on the task, trying to think of the young woman who continually slipped into his mind at the oddest moments. He was making her a birthday gift, he thought. Of course he'd be thinking of her.

He was surprised that he missed seeing her this morning. It shouldn't matter who came to sit with Jacob as long as he wasn't left alone.

Thoughts of Jacob reminded him that his brother had his follow-up appointment at noon. He hid the block and tools in a safe place before he headed to the house to wash up and change his clothes. He thanked God that he remembered the appointment before it was too late.

"Ellie, Jake has a noon doctor's appointment. We're going to head out now."

"I'll wait here until you come back," Charlie's sister said.

Nate smiled. "We shouldn't be too long."

"Jacob, your foot is healing," the doctor said. "The X-ray looks good. You should continue to stay off it as much as possible. It's still too early for the bone to knit."

"How long do I have to keep this boot on?" Jacob asked. His brother didn't like wearing it. He didn't see the need for it since he couldn't walk on it anyway.

"For a few weeks yet. I'd like you to come back in three weeks, when I'll take another X-ray." The man smiled. "You may walk with crutches but only if you're careful and only for very short periods of time."

Jacob looked pleased. "I'll be careful." As they left, he turned to Nate. "I'll have to wear this boot to Charlie's party," he said with a frown.

Nate opened the buggy door and helped his brother in. "You will, but it'll be fine. You can use the crutches as long as you don't overdo it."

"Why did I have to hear about the party

from Ellie? Why didn't you tell me? She said that you knew."

"I'd planned to tell you. I've had a lot on my mind." He paused. "And I wanted to make sure you were up for it."

"I'll be fine."

"*Ja*, you will," Nate replied. "I'm sorry I didn't mention it sooner."

"Ellie said the whole family's been invited. Do you think *Mam* and *Dat* will want to go?"

"I'm sure they will." The thought of celebrating Charlie's birthday with her family and giving his present to her gave Nate pleasure.

"I need to get her a gift. I don't know how I'll get out to buy one," Jacob said morosely.

"We've got time." He paused. "I'll go shopping for you."

His brother brightened. *"Danki."*

"Any ideas on what to buy?"

Jacob thought for a moment. Suddenly his features warmed as he grinned. "A board game."

"Life on the Farm?" Charlie and Jacob had been immersed in the game when he'd come in the fields on more than one day. She'd played the game before but she didn't own it.

"She'd like that."

"Life on the Farm it is, then." Nate steered

the horse toward home and passed a buggy along the way. He glanced over and froze.

"Is that Charlie?" Jacob asked.

"Looks like it."

"I wonder where she's going?"

"I have no idea. She didn't say what she'd be doing today." He frowned. She hadn't once glanced in their direction, which was odd because Charlie usually waved to everyone. Even him. Nate stifled the urge to go after her since Ellie was waiting for them at the house. He could drop Jacob off then look for Charlie. He couldn't shake the feeling that something was wrong.

Ellie had a meal waiting when they got to the house. Nate smiled his thanks as he helped his brother inside. He ate his peanut butter and jam sandwich then told Ellie and Jacob that he was headed to the store. After retrieving money from his room, he came downstairs to find the two immersed in a card game. When he told them he was leaving, they acknowledged him with a small hand wave but didn't look up. He grinned. The two would be kept busy for hours.

Her heart wasn't in the task as Charlie meandered about the grocery store, finding the food items her mother wanted. She still hadn't heard about the teaching job. Her meeting with Bishop John the other day hadn't gone all that well. She'd tried not to dwell on it, but she couldn't help but worry.

John Fisher had listened quietly while she'd told him why she wanted to teach, while she tried to convince him that she was the right person for the job. Unfortunately, Bishop John hadn't given her much hope. He'd been candid to the point where it'd felt painful, reminding her about a teacher's duty to lead her students by good example. As if he wondered if she could be a responsible adult in the classroom.

Would she never escape her past? She'd been young when she'd gotten into scrapes, and it'd been a long time since she'd started to think before acting. The more she thought about her visit to see John, the worse she felt about her chances of being hired.

Tears stung her eyes and she blinked them away. All was not totally lost. *Yet*. The bishop hadn't denied her the job outright. In fact, he'd told her the decision would be made by the church elders. What upset her was that John hadn't offered to give her a recommendation.

Charlie took a jar of blackstrap molasses from the store shelf and stared at it until the label blurred in her vision. She knew she'd be a great teacher, but she might never have the chance to show her community. She sniffed as she put the jar into her market basket then moved down the aisle.

"Charlie."

The deep, familiar voice startled her. "Nathaniel. I didn't expect to see you here."

He studied her intently. "Something's happened," he said. "What?"

"Nothing."

"'Tis not nothing." His voice was soft. "Tell me."

She blinked rapidly and wouldn't look at him. When his fingers touched her chin as he turned her gently to face him, she gasped.

"Charlie," he breathed.

She exhaled sharply. "I spoke with Bishop John about becoming teacher."

He nodded and waited for her to continue. Her skin warmed with his touch. "And what did he say?" he asked softly.

"That children needed to be led by a *gut* example," she said. "Then he reminded me about my bad behavior as a child and asked if I thought I could lead by *gut* example."

"And what did you tell him?"

"I told him I could." She scowled. "I'm not a child. I wish he'd see that. I know that students look up to their teacher. That if I'm teacher, they will look up to me. 'Tis a responsibility I'd take seriously."

Nate frowned. "Did he say that you wouldn't be considered?"

"Nay." She was shocked to realize that he was genuinely upset for her. His nearness, his disappointment on her behalf, gave her tremendous comfort. "He said it was up to the elders to make the final decision."

His brow cleared. "Then have faith that you may still get the job."

Her head began to pound. "I don't think so. He didn't offer to put in a *gut* word for me."

"How can he? If he did it for you, he'd have to do it for all the other candidates." He eyed her compassionately. "You shouldn't take it to heart. He's right. Our church elders will make the final decision and they'll consider every single person who has shown an interest." He briefly caressed her cheek before he withdrew.

"Every single person?" She groaned.

"I'm sure no one wants to be our new *schuul*teacher more than you. And believe it or not, that will work in your favor."

Her mouth curved. "I can't know that for certain." She was surprised when he reached for her hand. She stifled a gasp of pleasure at the simple touch.

She didn't want to pull away. The warmth of his skin against hers gave her goose bumps. She liked him holding her hand. Probably too much.

His gaze remained tender as he rubbed his thumb lightly across her wrist. She became overwhelmed with feelings she shouldn't have, with wishing that Nate would see her as someone he found attractive. A woman, not a child. She sighed but managed to control her wayward thoughts. "What are you doing here?"

He arched an eyebrow as he held up a list. "Buying food. The same as you."

She looked away. "Ellie doing well at the *haus*?"

"*Ja*. When I left, she and Jacob were playing cards."

Charlie stifled her disappointment. Apparently, neither Nate nor Jake had missed her.

"Will you be coming tomorrow?" he asked quietly, his blue eyes focused on her.

"Do you want me to?"

"Jacob will want you to come." He tore his gaze away to search the store aisle. "And I want you to come." She saw him study his list then examine the food items on the shelf in front of him. "Jake likes the way you challenge him. He said it's no fun to win every game. Ellie can't beat him like you can."

She allowed her lips to curve. "You mean, I'm *gut* at games other than baseball?"

Would she be as good of a teacher as she was a game-player? Her smile fell. She thought she'd be good at teaching, but she might never get the chance to prove it.

Nate selected an item from the shelf. As if he'd sensed her dismay, he abruptly faced her. "Charlie, stop worrying." He gave her shoulder a quick, reassuring squeeze. "We are here to shop. Since we're both here at the same time, why don't we shop together?"

She shrugged. "Why not?"

It was fun food-shopping with Nate. The man teased her every time she pulled merchandise off the shelf. He asked her what she needed it for, and if she was certain the item was exactly what she wanted. He was so outrageous in his comments that eventually all she could do was grin at him and razz him back.

Nate was handsome. She'd never known anyone with his particular shade of blue eyes. Nate's seemed to change colors to every available vibrant shade of blue. Every time their gazes met her heart fluttered.

She was setting herself up for heartbreak. She knew it but she couldn't regret the way he made her feel—giddy and happy and more alive than ever before. She knew that he'd never think of her in that way, but she didn't care. As long as she had a legitimate excuse to spend time with him, she could enjoy his company without fear that he'd guess she had feelings for him.

They meandered about the store together, selecting the items and placing them in their market baskets. Charlie helped Nate find everything he needed and suggested a few other items that she'd forgotten to include on his list. He bought whatever she told him to, which pleased her.

Charlie was feeling better by the time the cashier had rung up their purchases and they headed out the door. "I'll stay with Jacob," she said once Nate and she were outside in the sun. "If you really want me to."

His blue eyes flashed briefly. "I do."

She felt warm and shivery as they headed toward the hitching post behind the building where they'd parked their buggies. She loaded her grocery bags in the back of her vehicle, then faced him. "I'll see you tomorrow."

Nate hesitated. It seemed as if he wanted

to say more. "I'll tell Jake you'll be by in the morning," he finally said.

Disappointed, she climbed into her buggy, waved, then left for home, wishing she could have spent more time with him, wondering if he'd be around for her to see him tomorrow.

He watched as Charlie drove away before he climbed into his wagon. The sight of her tears earlier had ripped through him like fire. She was upset and he hated it. There was nothing he could do but he wished there was. She had forbidden him to talk with his deacon father about her desire to become teacher. But what if he spoke with someone else? He wouldn't be breaking his promise to her, and it might make a difference for her if he told John everything she'd been doing for him and Jacob. He knew Bishop John well. Would it really hurt for him to talk with the man?

He had to get back. Ellie waited for him. She was no doubt eager to go home.

Ellie sat alone at the kitchen table, sipping tea, when he carried in the groceries ten minutes later.

"Jacob's napping," she said when he entered the house.

"He *oll recht*?"

"*Ja*, he's fine. He was tired." She grinned.

"Probably of winning every single game." Her expression filled with concern. "He was hurting but wouldn't take his pain medication. I gave him aspirin with a mug of sweetened hot milk."

Nate smiled. *"Danki."* He started to unbag groceries. "Ellie, when I'm done putting these away, I'd like to run one more errand. It won't take long. I know you've been here all day."

"'Tis fine, Nate. Go ahead. I've no jobs today. I don't mind staying longer." She stood and reached for the other two bags. "Go. I'll put these away for you."

He beamed at her. "I'll be back soon."

A short time afterward Nate knocked on the bishop's door. It was John himself who answered. "Sally and Nicholas are sleeping," his friend and church elder said quietly after they'd greeted each other. "Come in." He gestured toward the kitchen table. "Want coffee?"

"I wouldn't mind a cup." Nate smiled his thanks when John shoved the sugar bowl and pitcher of milk toward him after he handed him a filled mug.

"Is this a social visit? Or do you have something on your mind?"

"Something on my mind," he admitted. "Actually, someone. Charlie Stoltzfus."

The bishop narrowed his gaze. "What trouble has the girl gotten into now?"

Nate nearly choked as he tried to swallow his sip of coffee. "*Nay*, you've got it wrong. Charlie hasn't been in trouble for years." And he suddenly realized the truth. He'd been telling himself that she was young and reckless, but that was a long time ago. He sighed, hoping this would make up for the way he'd misjudged her. "I heard she's interested in the teaching position at our *schuul*. I thought it might help for you to know a few things about her."

John leaned forward, looking interested. "The church elders have already selected a replacement, but tell me anyway."

Nate explained about Jacob's accident and Charlie's help. "She'd make a fine teacher," he said sincerely. "I'm sorry that I came too late."

The bishop smiled as he leaned back in his chair. "I'm glad to hear how you feel about her. She needs someone like you in her life."

"She's just a friend," Nate insisted, stiffening.

John nodded. "Still, I'm glad you came to tell me. 'Tis always nice to hear *gut* things about a church member." He rose and refilled his coffee cup. "The church elders have already made their choice. Unfortunately, I can't say until after we make an offer."

"I see." He rose. "I appreciate your time, John."

"We've known each other a long time. Your *dat* has been deacon for years. We're friends. I always make time for my friends and fellow church members." John followed him to the door. "And Nate? I didn't say it was too late. I said that the elders have made their choice."

Nate brightened with hope. "Do you mean...?"

"The elders have made their choice," the bishop said with a smile. "You'll find out after she does."

Nate offered up a silent prayer that Charlie would get her wish. The bishop made him wonder. If she didn't get the position, then he'd have to find a way to cheer her up. His parents would be home soon, and there would no longer be a reason for Charlie to return... unless his *mam* still wanted her to mind Mae and Harley. He was going to miss seeing her every day. A fact he'd have to get used to if she did become teacher with little time for babysitting or anything else.

He would make arrangements to buy that farm tomorrow. No sense in waiting. He had a future to plan...without Charlie. His pleasure dimmed as he pulled into the barnyard. Ellie was inside, waiting to go home. He wished it was Charlie in the house, then he could find an excuse to keep her awhile longer. Suddenly, he wanted to spend as much time as he could with her...before time ran out and she was gone.

He greeted Ellie as he entered the house. "Jacob still sleeping?"

"*Ja*, I have a feeling he'll be up soon." She grabbed her traveling cape. "You be *oll recht* if I head home?"

"We'll be fine."

Ellie smiled. She was a pretty woman with blond hair and blue eyes, but she didn't catch his interest as much as her sister did with her red hair and bright green eyes. "I have to work, but Charlie should be back tomorrow." She studied him for several long seconds. "If she can't come, I can ask Nell."

Nate stiffened but managed to smile. "We should be able to manage on our own."

"It might be best if Charlie comes until your *eldre* come home." She put on her traveling bonnet.

He felt his chest tighten. "You're probably right."

"She needs a man, Nate. Someone like you. Any suggestions?"

"Are you talking about Jacob?"

She shrugged. "Maybe. Maybe not. You know my sister. Do you think she and Jake would be happy together?" Ellie left then, leaving Nate stewing over the suggestion that his brother could make Charlie happy.

Was she suggesting that Charlie and Jacob would be a good match?

His mind rebelled at the thought, but there were worse prospects for Charlie's affection than Jacob. His brother was a good, kind man, and Charlie might be happy with him.

But how could he accept her as his sister-in-law when he wanted her for himself?

He and Jacob enjoyed a leftover supper that Charlie had prepared the day before. Nate studied his brother as Charlie's prospective husband. Jacob and Charlie got along well. They laughed and teased one another while they played games.

Charlie had tensed whenever Nate pulled up a chair to watch them play...until recently when he and she had enjoyed shopping together.

Nate sighed. He wanted to be the right man for Charlie but he wasn't. That night, as he stared at the ceiling, he considered every young man within their Amish community who could possibly be a good match for Charlie. One by one, he dismissed most of them as unsuitable. There were only two men who might be good enough for her—his brother Jacob and Matt Troyer, her brother-in-law's brother.

He hated the thought of her with either man.

He wanted to be the one who cared for her, teased her. He loved watching her eyes light up whenever she was happy.

Even if she married someone else, he'd get to see her on Sundays. It wasn't what he wanted, but it was something. Nate groaned and covered his eyes with his arm. He wanted to wed Charlie…but he was afraid. He felt the pain of knowing he'd failed in the past. He couldn't do it again. He couldn't fail Charlie as he'd failed Emma.

Chapter Eight

Saturday morning Charlie headed over to
the Peachy farm, her thoughts on the day
ahead. Something had happened between
her and Nate in the store yesterday. A turning point in their relationship, a warm kind
of friendship that she'd enjoyed, maybe
too much. He'd seemed to like her company as they'd shopped. They'd laughed as
they chose groceries and teased each other
whenever one of them picked something
off the shelf that they didn't need or want.
He'd made her feel better about her meeting with the bishop, but whatever happened,
she knew she'd get over it. Teaching wasn't
the only thing she could do. She could take
other work, perhaps working for Ellie cleaning houses.

The air had grown colder, reminding her

that it was nearly Christmas. She needed to decide what to give everyone. She could make something for her sisters, but it was harder to think of a gift for their husbands. For her parents, she'd buy something special. Maybe she'd make *Mam* a new apron, then she'd purchase a toy for the dog her father loved so much that he'd brought it in from the barn to live in the house.

Once again her thoughts turned to Nate, as they did a lot lately. She'd like to give him something—and to Jacob, too. She'd spent time with both of them this month, and they'd become friends. It just felt right to give a gift to her friend. Except she wanted more with Nate, although she'd never tell him unless he told her first that he felt the same way.

She pulled up to the house and climbed out. Nate came out of the barn and waved to her.

"Charlie!" His smile made her heart sing. "I'm glad you came." His face changed, filling with concern as he drew closer. "How are you?"

"I'm fine. No matter what happens I'll be fine."

Her breath caught when his mouth widened into a grin. "That's the best way to think. Have you had breakfast?" he asked, startling her.

"*Nay*, I thought I'd fix us something." She held up a plate. "And *Mam* sent muffins."

"I'd like to make you eggs."

She eyed him with shock. "You want to cook for me?"

He nodded. "You've done so much for us. I'd like to do something for you."

"You don't have to do that." She swallowed against a tight throat.

"I want to." His words made her heart beat more rapidly. He placed his hand at the small of her back as they walked toward the house together.

She halted at the back door. "Nathaniel, are you sick?"

He frowned. "*Nay*. Why do you ask?"

"You're being nice to me. You want to *cook* for me."

He shrugged but amusement glimmered in his blue eyes. "I'm sorry I've been such an ogre."

"*Nay*, I didn't mean that." She bit her lip, conscious of his nearness and loving every moment. "'Tis just that you like to—"

"Tease you?"

"I was going to say 'taunt' but I guess you were only teasing."

Nate bobbed his head. "I like teasing you."

She tilted her head as she gazed up at him. "Why?"

"Because you rise to the bait so quickly."

Understanding made her laugh. "I do, don't I?"

"*Ja*, you do."

They exchanged grins.

The new warmth in their relationship made her happy. "Well, now that I know, it's going to be harder to get a rise out of me."

"Will it?" he said as he reached around her to open the door.

The kitchen was warm and bright as the sun shone through the windows—one over the sink and one next to the back entrance.

Nate gestured toward the kitchen table. "Have a seat."

Charlie studied him. "Why do you want to feed me?"

"I told you… I want to do something nice for you."

"Wouldn't it have been easier to buy me an ice cream?"

His dark eyes gleamed. "You like ice cream? Perhaps another day after the weather warms again." Then something in his gaze clouded, and Charlie understood. She would no longer be around him then. He and she would never eat ice cream or do anything else together after his parents came home.

Jacob used crutches as he entered the kitchen from the other room. "*Gut* morning, Charlie."

She smiled at him warmly. "How are you feeling?"

"Better," he said as he pulled out a chair and sat down. His brows rose as he watched his brother take eggs out of the refrigerator and place a pan on the stove. "You're making breakfast?"

She shrugged when she met Jacob's gaze. "Apparently, he wants to do something *nice* for me."

Jacob's eyes narrowed as he turned back to his brother. "You want to do something nice for Charlie?" he asked doubtfully.

Without deviating from the task, Nate nodded. "And you."

Jacob leaned close to her ear. "I wonder what's come over him?"

She laughed. "I asked if he was sick," she whispered. Nate spun to gaze at them through narrowed eyes. She grinned at him. "Your *bruder* is wondering what's come over you," she told him.

He stared at his brother. "I've cooked for you before."

"True, but not when there was a woman in the kitchen."

"*Mam* was near."

"That's different."

Nate scowled. "I want to do something nice for her. What's wrong with that?"

Charlie regarded him softly. "Nothing, Nathaniel. Nothing at all. In fact, I like it." She smirked. "I might expect it more often."

His gaze grew tender. "We'll see, little one."

She frowned. Was he reminding her of their age difference? As far as she was concerned, there was no difference.

"What do you have to do today, Nate?" Jacob asked.

"Just a few farm chores and there's work to be done inside."

Charlie jerked as she stared at him. "You don't need me to stay."

"*Ja*, I do," he assured her. "I need someone to keep an eye on this one. If not, he's liable to get into trouble."

She relaxed. "Can't get into trouble if we're playing Aggravation."

Jacob laughed. "You mean if I beat you at every game we play."

"You wish." Charlie sensed Nate's gaze on her. She saw a flicker of emotion that he quickly masked.

He set a plate of scrambled eggs, sausage and toast before her and Jacob. "Enjoy," he said huskily before he turned back to the stove. She watched as he washed up the utensils and pans he used and set them to drain.

"Aren't you joining us?" she asked as he started to dry and put everything away.

"No time," Nate said.

She didn't understand. Then why did he stop to fix her breakfast? Nathaniel Peachy was a confusing man. A kind and complex man, who was thoughtful and wonderful, and she liked him. But there were times she didn't understand him at all. She stood to help him.

"Sit," he ordered. "Eat before your food gets cold."

"Nate."

"You've got games to play and I have work to do."

She eyed him with concern. "Nate. Is something bothering you?"

His smile didn't quite reach his blue gaze. "I'm fine."

Charlie nodded and let him be. There was nothing else she could do. She watched him leave the room and heard him go upstairs. If she knew what had upset him, maybe she could help.

Jacob was clearly enjoying the breakfast

that Nate had made for him. He seemed oblivious to his brother's mood, and he had always impressed her as a man who was quick with his concern.

Moments later Nate entered the kitchen on his way out the door. "I thought I'd go to the store first. Anything either of you need?"

Charlie shook her head. "I'm fine." She experienced a sniggle of uneasiness when he didn't look at her. "Didn't you buy everything you needed yesterday?"

He met her gaze. "I wouldn't be going to the store if I had, would I?"

His sharp tone made her stomach burn as the brothers exchanged looks before Nate left. She watched him go with a disturbing feeling of loss. She shouldn't feel this way. It wasn't as if she had his affection to begin with.

Jacob reached for his coffee. "Aggravation, Dutch Blitz or Life on the Farm?" There was a twinkle and challenge in his blue eyes so like his brother's.

She managed to laugh. "Doesn't matter. You pick. I'll trounce you in whatever we play."

Nate climbed into his buggy, his heart aching. Charlie and Jacob got along well together. His brother was a good man, and while it would kill him to see them married and with children, he understood that Jacob would make Charlie a good husband. Not that he would shove Jake in Charlie's direction. He would step back and watch it happen…and deal with the pain of seeing it all take place.

He steered his horse toward the new general store just outside Happiness. The shop had a great hardware section and he needed a new doorknob for his sister's bedroom. On the way there, he passed the farm he wanted to purchase and decided to stop and speak with the owner to make an offer on the land. To his delight, the man accepted it. Pleased, Nate continued to the store, then shopped with heightened spirits. He easily found what he needed then meandered through the rest of the shop looking for something for Jacob to give Charlie for her birthday. He still had work to do on the horse he'd carved for her, but there was time yet to finish it up.

He looked for the game aisle and finally saw all of their Amish community favorites. The only game that Charlie didn't have was Life on the Farm. He grabbed the box and continued down the row. He wished he could think of another gift for Charlie, something special. What if she didn't like the hand-carved figure?

His thoughts grew dark as he completed his purchase. Why should it matter whether or not she liked his gift? It wasn't as if she'd ever belong to him. She'd find a suitor and marry someone else. He scowled. Jacob.

The air stayed chilly and he knew he'd have to think about Christmas sooner than expected. As he drove toward home, he forced his feelings for Charlie from his mind and made a mental list of the tasks that needed to be done today. He needed to paint the outside window he'd recently replaced but the temperature was too cold. He'd fix his sister's bedroom doorknob, then tackle the various other items that needed to be done inside. He didn't really want to work in the house. Watching Charlie and Jacob together made his gut wrench.

A half hour later, as Nate worked on replacing the door, Charlie exited his room with a basket of laundry. "What are you doing?" he snapped irritably.

She halted and stared at him. "The wash."

"You don't have to do mine."

He saw hurt flash in her pretty green eyes and felt mean. "I've been doing it for nearly a week, Nate," she said quietly. "I like washing clothes." She paused and her face turned pale. "You don't want me to touch your garments."

He closed his eyes and struggled to soften his tone. "You don't have to."

"I know," she said and started toward the stairs.

His thoughts in turmoil, he returned to the work, turned the screwdriver one last time to tighten it and cried out as his tool slipped with the end digging into his finger.

Charlie was suddenly beside him, her expression concerned, her laundry basket on the floor next to her. "What happened?"

"A bit of an accident. I'm fine."

She gazed down at the redness of his injury and grabbed his other hand. "Downstairs now."

The last thing he needed or wanted was to be this close to Charlie. *"Nay,"* he snapped. "I said I'm fine."

She jerked as if struck. "I see." She retrieved the laundry basket and started to descend the stairs, pausing on one to scold, "I wasn't expecting anything from you, Nathaniel Peachy. I would have offered to help anyone!"

Then she left him standing in the hallway, his heart aching, his chest hurting. He put the screwdriver away, then waited a moment to get his emotions under control. He heard the washer lid slam, realized that even while angry, she had put his dirty laundry in to wash. With a sigh of regret, Nate went down to check on Jacob. His brother was asleep. Apparently, Charlie's fit of temper, although justified, hadn't disturbed Jacob in the least.

Wound tighter than a metal coil, Nate drew in a calming breath then entered the kitchen. She barely looked at him as she prepared a meal on the stove. Feeling properly chastened, he left the house for the barn. Where he had things to do, he assured himself. Finishing Charlie's present was just one of them.

A light snow fell Sunday morning as Charlie and her family climbed into their buggy and headed toward church service. Her cousin Elijah and his wife, Martha, were hosting today. *Mam* and Ellie had fixed side dishes for the shared community meal after church. Before she'd left the Peachy house yesterday, she had made a bowl of macaroni salad for Nate and Jacob to bring. The macaroni salad had turned out well. Jacob had tasted it and proclaimed it delicious while threatening to eat every bit. Coming in from outside, Nate had gazed at the huge bowl then studied her with a thoughtful look that made her uncomfortable. Tension had hung in the air between them, bringing her to the verge of tears, but she managed not to cry. At his brother's urging, Nate had tasted it then given her a compliment. As his small praise raised her spirits, she'd realized that she was deeply affected by his moods.

Cradling a dried apple pie, Charlie stared out the window as her father drove the buggy. The scent of cinnamon and apples drifted to her nose, tempting her to take a taste, but she didn't. She couldn't eat even if she wanted to. She felt butterflies at the prospect of seeing Nate. Maybe later, after service, she'd feel well enough to eat.

She enjoyed church as she looked around Elijah and Martha's great room, happy to see her family and friends and neighbors. Across the room in the men's section sat Jacob and Nathaniel. Nate held his brother's arm as Jacob stood, propped up on his crutches. Jacob glanced over at her and smiled. Her lips curved before her gaze settled on his older brother. As if sensing her study, Nate locked gazes with her. She caught her breath as she nodded then turned away. Heart racing wildly, she joined in to sing another hymn from the *Ausbund*. And silently prayed to get what she wanted most. The teaching job and a life with Nate.

Bishop John Fisher spoke during the service, followed by Preacher Levi. When it was over, Charlie joined the women in bringing out the food for the shared meal. She heard talk of her cousins organizing a baseball team. Normally, Charlie would have been eager to join in. But not this day. If she wanted to be teacher and to earn others' respect, she needed to be responsible and act her age. When Isaac came looking for her to play, she politely declined with the excuse that she wasn't up to it today. The day was warmer than it had been yesterday. When she peeked through the window to see how the game was going, she saw the young men of the community wearing their long white shirts with their black Sunday best vests and pants. The last thing she should do was play baseball in her Sunday best dress and slide in the dirt to score a home run. Her mother would tolerate it, simply because she was a loving parent, but *Mam* wouldn't be happy if her good clothes got dirty or ripped.

She turned away from the sight and gasped. Nate Peachy stood behind her with a tense look on his handsome face. "What's wrong? Is it Jacob?"

The man shook his head. "Jacob's fine." He was silent as he moved toward the window and glanced outside. "Why aren't you play-ing baseball?"

Charlie gave him a twisted smile. "Not feeling up to it. Besides, I'm wearing my church clothes and *Mam* won't appreciate it if I play in them." And she knew he didn't approve.

He turned from the window to study her intently. A small smile curved his lips. "I sup-pose she wouldn't."

"Jacob must be disappointed that he can't play."

"I'm sure he is but he'll get back to it even-tually."

As she joined him at the window, Charlie sighed, for she had a feeling that her baseball-playing days were over.

"Charlie—" His voice rumbled from beside her. There was something so private about standing so close to him.

She met his gaze. *"Ja?"*

He shook his head.

She frowned. "Your family will be home soon?"

"Ja. I got a message that my *grossmudder* is doing better. They'll be home this week."

"I see." She knew a sharp disappointment.

"I appreciate all you've done for us."

The gratitude in his gaze bothered her. "It wasn't any trouble."

"Charlie!" a familiar voice called from across the room.

"My sister's demanding my attention. I guess *Mam* and *Dat* are ready to leave." She forced a smile. "I'll see you tomorrow." *Unless you don't want me.* She started to walk away then stopped after Nate gently clasped her arm.

"Danki," he said softly with heartfelt thanks.

"Charlie!" Ellie called, waving her to come.

"I've got to go." She walked a few steps then halted to face him. Her face warmed at the look in his eyes. "I'll see you tomorrow." Then she flashed him a grin and left. Snow started to fall as her father steered their buggy home.

The next morning, bright and early after doing her chores, Charlie arrived at the Peachy residence. Yesterday's snow lay across the ground like a transparent white blanket. She entered the house, and Nate murmured a quick greeting to her before he left her alone to spend time with Jacob. She didn't mind. Jacob was good company and despite how frustrating it must be for him with the boot on his foot, he was pleasant and fun to be with.

Which didn't mean she didn't long to spend time with Nate.

Nate didn't come in for lunch. She knew he was working in the barn so she made him a sandwich and poured him a cup of coffee, then headed out to give it to him while Jake tucked in for a nap.

She felt a burst of nervous excitement as she carried Nate's lunch across the yard. Yesterday he'd wanted her here.

It was dark inside the barn when she entered. Not wanting to frighten him, Charlie called out. "Nate! I've brought you something to eat!"

He popped his head up over one of the barn stalls. "Charlie. What are you doing here?"

His brow furrowed, he sounded annoyed.

An ache settled within her chest. "I brought you lunch. I know you're busy." She set the plate and cup on a table outside a stall several yards away. "I'll just leave it here." Her throat felt tight. She was just trying to do something nice for him. She spun to leave. "I'll see you later."

She had taken only a few steps when he was beside her. "Charlie." She looked up at him, saw tenderness in his expression. She blinked, sure it would be gone when she gazed at him again. To her astonishment, he reached out to cup her cheek. "You brought me lunch."

She nodded, aware of the way her skin tingled where he touched her. "I wasn't sure, but I thought you might be hungry."

He smiled as she stepped back, and she felt the loss of his warmth. "I am. *Danki.*"

She hesitated. It was none of her business what he was doing, but she admitted to herself that she was curious. "Do you need any help?"

He frowned. "Where's Jacob?"

"Resting."

Nate shook his head. "I'm managing fine, Charlie. You should get back inside in case Jacob needs you."

She walked away, feeling as if she'd been scolded. Then anger lit a fire in her, and she spun. "You know something, Nathaniel Peachy? I don't know what to say or how to act around you! You can be wonderfully kind one minute then cold and unfeeling the next!"

Then she turned and hurried out, blinded by tears. So she'd told him off. So what? It wasn't as if she'd had a prayer that he'd want a relationship with her. Still, as she ran toward the house, she prayed that she would be proven wrong and that Nate would one day see her as someone he could love and marry.

She sniffed. She shouldn't want that, but she couldn't help herself. Her heart wanted him, and she couldn't control it.

Nate returned to the house not long after she did. She was embarrassed by her early outburst. "You can head home," he said gruffly.

And so she left. She wondered if he'd want her back but she didn't ask, certain that he was angry enough to want her to stay away.

Her mother looked relieved to see her when she got home. *"Gut!"* she exclaimed. *"Endie* Katie has invited us for supper, and I was afraid you'd be late. She wants to pick holly and cut pine for Christmas after we eat."

Charlie frowned. "It's only three o'clock."

"She invited us for four thirty," *Mam* said.

"Plenty of time." Enough for her to put on clean clothes. "Is Ellie home?"

"Ja. She came home at noon."

She nodded. "I'm going upstairs and wash up a bit."

"How is Jacob?"

"Gut. He's doing much better."

"When are Abram and Charlotte due back?"

"Any day." Abram's wife, Charlotte King Peachy, had the same first name as hers, which was why everyone within the community called her Charlie since her family's move to Happiness, her father's boyhood home, years ago. She didn't mind the nickname; she was young then, and the name had seemed to fit.

They headed toward her aunt Katie's shortly after. She wondered why they were going so early, but then she recalled that the days were getting shorter, and she figured that her father didn't want to drive in the dark. Just last week he'd heard about a terrible buggy accident toward New Holland. It had been dark, and the family had put on their running lights; yet, a car had come up from behind them and hit them, forcing the vehicle off the road. Sometimes one had to go out in the dark, but still it made one think twice after hearing of such a terrible accident. All four Amish members had been hospitalized. They had survived but with serious injuries. Bishop John had mentioned them during church yesterday and asked everyone to remember them in their prayers. Charlie had. She'd thought about them this morning and asked the Lord to grant them a speedy recovery.

There were three other buggies in the Samuel Lapp barnyard when they arrived.

"Your cousins," her mother told her before she could ask.

Charlie smiled. She couldn't wait to see her cousins and their wives. She saw them at church service, but there was never enough time to do more than briefly chat with them. Ellie climbed out of the buggy first and grabbed the pie from her.

"I don't know about you, but I'm hungry," her sister said.

"I could eat." Charlie climbed out and reached for the pie. Ellie shook her head and told her she'd carry it in.

The door swung open as Charlie climbed the porch steps, reaching it first. "Charlie!" Her cousin Hannah grinned at her. She was the youngest member of the Lapp family and the only daughter in a family of eight children. "Come in!" The girl glanced over her shoulder. "Charlie's here!" she called.

Suddenly, she was being dragged into the great room, where she faced a mass of familiar faces. "Surprise!" everyone called. "Happy birthday!"

Charlie felt her jaw drop as shock rendered her speechless. Her married sisters, Nell, Meg and Leah, were there with their husbands. All of her cousins were present as well as the Zooks, the Troyers and the Kings. She experienced a jolt of pleasure when her gaze encountered Nate Peachy, who stood next to Jacob, steadying his brother on crutches. He smiled and mouthed "Happy birthday."

Behind the brothers was their family, who must have returned within the last hour. She suffered a heavy heart as she forced herself to smile brightly. There would be no more time with Jacob. *No more time with Nate.*

"Are you *oll recht*?" Nell asked. As if sensing something wrong, her eldest sister had approached silently from behind.

She nodded, still without speaking. Everyone was looking at her, and she was the center of attention, this time not because of trouble but for something good. Still, it wasn't happy she felt. It was sadness because of Nate. But she would force herself to be happy for her aunt and uncle and everyone who had come to celebrate her birthday.

"First time I've known Charlie to be speechless!" her cousin Isaac called out.

Everyone laughed. Charlie, face red, eyed her cousin. "Don't get used to it, Isaac!" she shot back, which made everyone roar with laughter. Even Nate Peachy laughed and looked amused.

"Food's ready," her aunt declared, and everyone dispersed.

Her father approached and studied her warmly. "Nineteen. My youngest *dochter* is nineteen. 'Tis hard to believe."

"Because I still act as I did when I was fourteen?"

He shook his head. "*Nay*, because you're a woman now and I want to keep my little girl."

"Ah, *Dat.*" She became emotional.

Her father drew a sharp breath. "I'm not ready for you to marry."

Charlie jerked. "Who says I'll marry?"

"You will when the right man comes along," her mother said as she slipped her arm around her waist.

"I doubt anyone would be brave enough to take me on," Charlie said drily.

"By some of the looks you've been getting today, I can tell you you're mistaken." *Mam* nodded toward the corner of the room. "Jacob Peachy seems fond of you."

She smiled. "Jacob and I are *gut* friends." And it wasn't Jacob who had grabbed her interest; it was his older brother. An impossible situation.

"Charlie, come and eat," her cousin Hannah urged.

"I'm coming." Her mother released her and joined her father. Hannah grabbed her arm and tugged her toward the food table in the kitchen. Charlie glanced back and saw her parents' amusement with Hannah as they followed them into the other room.

They ate a delicious meal of Charlie's favorite foods—fried chicken, mashed potatoes, corn, coleslaw, fresh yeast rolls and fried apples. After filling their plates with food, everyone moved back to the great room to eat. Charlie stood off to the side, picking at her meal while watching everyone in the room. She'd been greatly moved that her aunt would host a birthday party for her, that everyone had come and seemed to be having a good time. *Nineteen.* She was nineteen years old, and she had yet to figure out what she would do with her life if she didn't manage the next step, which was to be teacher at their Happiness School. Today was for celebration, she reminded herself. Not for contemplating all the reasons that she wasn't going to get the job.

Someone approached from her left side— Matt Troyer, her brother-in-law James Pierce's half-brother. "Aren't you going to open your presents?" he asked with a grin.

Charlie shook her head as horror clutched her chest. She didn't want to open presents in front of everyone. "'Tis not my birthday until Wednesday," she reasoned.

Her gaze swept across the room, zooming in on Nate Peachy, the man who'd stolen her heart and made her breath catch. Matt hadn't moved. He watched her with a glimmer of admiration. She was flattered, but she didn't need his attention as other than a friend.

She turned her head to find Nate studying her. His expression was unreadable.

"Is there cake?" she asked Matt. "I love cake. Don't you?"

Charlie continued to feel Nate's gaze as she and Matt left the room for the kitchen, where cake, pies and a number of other desserts sat out on the counter.

Chapter Nine

Nate watched Charlie with Matt Troyer and endured a painful squeezing in his chest. Jacob, Matt… Who else noticed and appreciated Charlie Stoltzfus? He had no right to be upset—or to be jealous. She needed a man her own age, someone she could rely on, and it looked as if there were a number of potential beaus vying for her affection.

"Aren't you going to eat?" Jacob asked, eyeing Nate's plate. "You've barely touched your food."

He shrugged as he dug into his mashed potatoes with a fork. "Not hungry. You want to eat mine?"

"*Nay.* I have room enough for dessert." His brother grinned. "I want some of Charlie's birthday cake."

Nate caught his brother eyeing Charlie with a smile. "Doesn't it bother you?"

Jacob frowned. "What?"

"Seeing Charlie and Matt together."

He made a dismissive sound. "They are in-laws," Jacob said. "Besides, Charlie and I are just friends."

And heading toward something more, Nate thought with a grimace.

Hannah approached them with a look of displeasure. "Charlie won't open her gifts. She said it's not her birthday yet."

"Want me to talk with her?" Jacob offered.

"Would you?" The young teen looked up at him with a glimmer of hero worship.

Nate sighed. "Leave her be. I think she's uncomfortable with all of the attention." He sympathized with her. He wouldn't have been comfortable being the center of attention, either. Fortunately, he didn't have to worry about anyone throwing him a surprise birthday party. He was too old for one.

"I can still try if you want," Jacob said, although he seemed to understand and appreciate what Nate was telling him.

Hannah shook her head. "*Nay.* We'll let her open her gifts on her birthday." She paused. "At home."

Nate saw Charlie exit the kitchen with a

small plate and a huge grin on her face. Matt said something to make her chuckle as she pushed a fork into a piece of frosted angel food cake. She lifted a bite of cake to her mouth and placed it daintily between her lips. He watched as she chewed and swallowed, then as she murmured something that made Matt laugh.

Unable to stop himself, Nate approached. "Is that angel food cake?" he asked with a gentle smile.

He saw Charlie stiffen as Matt answered, "*Ja*, with maple syrup whipped cream." He took a quick bite then finished, "Charlie's favorite cake."

Matt saw someone across the room and he excused himself to talk with Barbara Zook, Annie Lapp's younger sister.

Nate was surprised to see Charlie blush. Because she was embarrassed over her enjoyment of cake? When she wouldn't look at him directly, he reached for her plate. "You'll share, won't you?"

Charlie's eyes shot daggers, and Nate chuckled. "I wouldn't steal your cake, Charlie." He eyed her with warmth. "Unless you wanted me to."

Her brows drew together in confusion. He gave in to the urge and swiped his finger to grab a dollop of whipped cream off her plate. He closed his eyes as he brought it up to his mouth and tasted. "Delicious."

"Don't," she warned him when he reached for more whipped cream.

He grinned at her. She stared at him in shock, then comprehension. "You're teasing me."

He nodded. "You said I couldn't get another rise out of you."

"You like it?"

"*Ja*. Who made it?"

"My sister Nell. She knows it's my favorite. It wouldn't be my birthday celebration without angel food cake with maple syrup whipped cream."

The two of them stood alone. Matt hadn't come back, and Nate was miffed with him. Clearly, he wasn't the right man for Charlie. He'd abandoned her for Barbara.

"You should get a piece," she told him, "before it's gone."

Nate saw Matt heading in their direction from across the room. "*Ja*, I suppose I should," he said politely as Matt joined them with a smile. He didn't feel any better with Matt's return.

There'd be no birthday cake for Nate. He'd lost what little appetite he'd had. *Happy birth-*

day, Charlie. She was a lovely woman. Not a girl—a woman, and he'd been making excuses about their age difference when he knew the real reason was Emma…and his past.

It was still light outside, but it wouldn't be for long. Needing some fresh air, Nate slipped out of the house to take a walk. When he returned inside, he accidentally overheard a conversation between Charlie and her sisters.

"Jacob's been paying you a lot of attention," Ellie said, teasing Charlie.

"So has Matt Troyer," Meg added with a smile.

"You have a number of handsome young men interested in you," Nell said.

Charlie waved them off. "Don't be ridiculous. They're my friends. They're not interested in me in that way."

Nate closed his eyes as he turned away. He had seen the way the men regarded Charlie. Did she really not see their interest? He scowled. She could have her pick of them whenever she wanted.

He slipped outside again. This time snow was falling as he escaped to the barn to seek solace in the silence of a familiar place. The sounds of the farm animals shifting around, the noises they made individually, soothed him. He didn't know how long he was there, but when he came outside it was past dusk and the snow was heavier. He spied someone standing near the fence, watching the horses that had yet to be brought in. *Charlie.*

Pulled in her direction, he approached, noting the slump of her slim shoulders. "Charlie," he murmured softly so as not to scare her. He slipped in to rest against the fence beside her. "Needed a few moments alone?" he asked when she didn't say anything.

She looked up at him with glistening green eyes and nodded. "It's a little overwhelming in there."

He stifled the strongest urge to pull her into his arms for comfort. He leaned against the fence rail and gazed ahead, waiting, hoping that she'd say something.

"What's wrong?" Nate asked.

"Nothing." How could she explain that she found her feelings for him confusing, terrifying yet somehow exciting?

"We're friends, aren't we?" he said gruffly. "You can tell me anything."

She glanced at him. "Are we friends, Nate? After today, I wasn't sure."

"Because my parents are back?"

"Nay!" she exclaimed, no longer able to keep silent. "I told you off."

"Oh, that." He seemed unconcerned.

She gaped at him. "It didn't bother you?"

He shrugged. "Why? Because you were honest with me?"

Charlie averted her gaze. She hadn't been honest about her true feelings for him.

"So, tell me. What did you decide? Jacob or Matt? Both are *gut* men—"

She stiffened and glared at him. "You didn't just dare to ask me that," she said tightly. She swung back to the view, her heart hammering in her chest, her muscles taut with anger. *Calm down*, she told herself. *Please, Lord, anger is a sin. Forgive me and help me to be a better person.*

A lengthy silence ensued. "I'm sorry," he said. "'Tis none of my business."

Closing her eyes, she drew in a cleansing breath, released it. "You're correct. 'Tis none of your business, but…" She forced herself to relax. "I shouldn't have snapped at you."

Their gazes locked. When Nate smiled, Charlie felt her fierce attraction for him from her head to her toes. Trembling, she faced ahead, lest Nate somehow read what was in her heart.

They stood side by side at the fence as

darkness descended. Their moments became peaceful, and Charlie was able to relax and enjoy his company. The little bit of time she'd have left with him.

No one came looking for them, which was a miracle to Charlie, clearly provided by the Lord, perhaps for her birthday. A goose honked overhead, the lone bird soaring high on a quest to find its flock.

Snow fell quietly, landing on her black coat and on Nate's jacket and bare head. His warmth surrounded her. He stood at her side as if he, too, felt enjoyment in the moment.

"I'm glad your family is home safe. I guess I won't be seeing you, except on Sundays."

"Charlie…"

She met his gaze, surprised to see a strange look in his eyes. "I appreciate all you've done." He reached out.

Charlie stilled as he brushed his fingers across her brow before he tucked a stray lock of hair behind her ear. "I didn't mind," she said hoarsely.

"Nate? Are you out here?" Charlie immediately recognized the voice as his sister Ruth Ann's. "Jake's foot is bothering him, and *Mam* and *Dat* think we should head home."

"I'll be right there," he called back. He gave her a wry smile. "I guess 'tis time for us to go. They're all tired. I'm surprised that they wanted to come." His voice grew husky. "I'm glad they did."

She didn't say anything. She studied his handsome features, his lit blue eyes, his firm jaw and devastating smile, and she experienced a longing so sharp it stole her breath.

He didn't move; he simply gazed at her. "Happy birthday, Charlie."

She smiled. "My birthday isn't until Wednesday."

Nate touched her cheek then stepped back. "Close enough."

As he turned and headed toward the house, Charlie felt her heart soften and leave with him. She wanted more from him, and she had to accept that she'd never have the relationship she wanted. She didn't follow him. She stayed at the fence and watched two of her uncle's horses cavort in the snow. It was flurrying out when minutes later Nate exited the house with Jacob and his family.

Seeing her, Jacob hobbled his way on crutches toward her. "Happy birthday, Charlie," he said with a pained smile.

"Go home and rest, Jacob."

Charlotte Peachy, Nate's stepmother, broke from the group and approached. "Happy birthday, Charlie." Her smile was warm. "*Danki* for taking such good care of my sons."

She could only smile in response. The woman placed a hand on her arm and gave it a squeeze before she rejoined her family.

She followed her to their buggy, where the man she loved waited. Nate helped his mother and brother get in and waited while the rest of his family was settled with his father in the front passenger seat before he faced Charlie. "Here. There's a gift in the house from my family, but this one is from me."

With trembling fingers, she took something wrapped up in a piece of linen, probably a pillowcase. "Nate…"

"Happy nineteenth birthday, Charlie," he whispered. Then he climbed into the buggy and within seconds he was driving with his family down the street toward home.

Charlie stood in the barnyard, watching as they left, clutching Nate's gift in her hands. It was true that she hadn't wanted to open the gifts until her birthday, but it was different with this one. This one was from Nate, and she had to open it now.

She moved into the barn, where no one would see her if they came looking. It would only take a moment to see what he'd given her, then she'd head into the house. She unwrapped Nate's gift and gasped with pleasure. It was a wooden carving of a horse. A perfect, smooth figure that looked alive and ready to prance if she set it on the ground. Emotional, she turned the figure, noting the detail and the tiny NP carved into the underside of one leg. NP. Nate Peachy. It was the best gift she'd ever been given. She loved horses, and Nate had noticed. She would cherish the little wooden horse forever, even after their paths went in different directions. She'd never forget that he'd taken the time to make something special for her birthday.

Charlie smiled with happiness even as tears filled her eyes and trailed down her cheeks. *Happy birthday to me.*

She hid the horse under the backseat in her family's buggy, ready to retrieve later when no one was around to see. Nate's gift would be for her eyes only. She would hold it, a precious thing, and recall the night he'd given it to her and all the times she'd enjoyed in his company.

The next morning while making coffee, Nate wondered if Charlie had opened his gift and if she'd liked it. He loved her. It was wrong but he couldn't help how he felt. The solution, he realized, was to keep his distance and move on with his life.

Chapter Ten

"Bishop John," Missy Stoltzfus greeted. "Come in. I'll make you a cup of coffee?" She stepped aside to allow the man to enter the house. "What brings you to see us this morning?"

"Your *dochter* Charlie. Is she in?" he said as he took a seat at the kitchen table.

"Is who in?" Charlie said as she entered the room. It was the day before she would turn nineteen, and the first day she had no reason to see Nate. She tensed as she saw their visitor. "Bishop John."

"Charlie, just the one I'm here to see."

She swallowed hard. *"Ja?"* Had he come to tell her about the new teacher?

"Since you expressed an interest in the position, I thought I should come and tell you that the church elders made their choice for our new *schuul*teacher."

She nodded as she sat down across the table from him with a lump in her throat. She watched her mother set a cup of coffee before the bishop, then nodded when her parent offered her a cup. "So who got the job?"

"I'm hoping you'll understand their choice." Bishop John studied her thoughtfully. "I didn't know how much you wanted the position."

"I didn't make it clear?"

"I see that it's clear enough now how much you want to teach."

"Ja." She looked away as her throat thickened and she fought back tears. She didn't get the job. "Who's the new teacher? Barbara Zook?" Barbara Zook was her brother-in-law Peter's sister. She had recently returned to Happiness after a long period of absence spent out of state with her grandparents.

The bishop shook his head. "There were a number of young women considered."

Charlie waited patiently although everything inside her wanted to scream for him to hurry up and tell her, so that she could have a good cry in her room.

"Charlie, the church elders have decided

that you should be teacher if you still want the job."

She blinked. Her mouth gaped open. She drew and released a sharp breath. "Me?"

He nodded, his eyes crinkling with good humor. "*Ja.* Do you still want the job?"

"*Ja.*" She'd grabbed on to the opportunity since she couldn't have what she wanted most—Nate's love.

Bishop John grinned. "'Tis settled, then. You are now officially the new teacher for our Happiness *schuul.*"

There was only one person she was eager to tell, because she knew he'd be pleased for her. Nate Peachy. Thinking of him made her rise abruptly. "I'm sorry, Bishop John, but I have to leave." She paused. "I'll come by your house later for details? When will I start?"

"The week before Christmas. Elizabeth Troyer will be moving with her family that Saturday and will be done teaching on Friday."

She bobbed her head with excitement. That was in just over a week. "I'll be there then before *schuul* starts at eight."

The man looked satisfied. "*Gut.*"

"*Mam,*" she said, turning toward her mother. "I need to run an errand." She grabbed her coat then headed toward the door. "Bishop John?"

The man looked at her.

"*Danki.* I won't let you or the church elders down."

He smiled. "I know you won't." He waved her toward the door. "You'd better go and tell whoever you have to tell."

Blushing, she nodded, put on her coat then ran out the door. Several minutes later she was on her way to the Peachy house. The day was clear, but the nip of winter was in the air. She tugged up on her coat to better protect her neck. She was almost there. She grinned, eager to see Nate and tell him her good news.

She parked in the yard, went to the back entrance and knocked before opening it. *"Hallo?"*

"Charlie!" Nate's stepmother came out from the laundry room. "'Tis nice to see you. Did you enjoy the party?"

She nodded. "It was truly a surprise," she said with a smile. She looked about, hoping for a sight of Nate, eager to tell him the good news.

Charlotte Peachy smiled at her with genuine affection. "I hear that you've been keeping Jacob company." She gestured toward a kitchen chair. "Tea?"

"Nay, but I appreciate the offer." She smiled.

"And Jacob and Nate needed help. I was happy to give it."

"You kept the *haus* clean."

She shrugged. "Needed a way to keep busy while Nate worked and Jacob slept."

"I appreciate it. I didn't know what I'd find when we returned."

Charlie smiled. "It must be *gut* to be home."

"*Ja*. We had a lovely time, but I missed being here. I enjoyed meeting Abram's *eldre*, though. They are wonderful people. I knew they would be given that they'd raised my wonderful husband to be the fine man that he is."

"Is Nate around?" she asked, feeling uncomfortable for asking.

"*Nay*. He went grocery-shopping."

"I want to talk with him, but I can come back another time."

"Do you want to leave him a message?"

"*Nay*. But if Jacob's awake, I'd like to say a quick *hallo*."

Nate's stepmother beamed her approval. "He is. I'm sure he'll be glad to see you. He's talked about all the games you've played together while we were gone."

"I suppose he told you he won most of them."

To her surprise, Nate's *mam* shook her

head. "Actually, he confessed that you beat him most of the time."

Charlie grinned. "An honest man. I like that." She hurried into the great room, where she found Jacob with a book open on his lap. "I just wanted to say *hallo* before I head home."

"You're leaving?" Jacob appeared disappointed.

"Your family's home. I didn't plan to stay."

"Play one game with me."

"*Nay*, you have siblings to play games with you now. I need to get home. There are chores to be done. I'll see you on Sunday."

"*Danki* for spending time with me," Jacob said warmly. "I'll have to sharpen my game skills before we play again."

"It was a hardship staying with you, Jake," she retorted mockingly, which made him grin.

She left then, disappointed and sad that her daily time spent with the two brothers was over. She climbed into her buggy and headed home. She had no idea where Nate had gone shopping, and she couldn't spend hours looking for him. She'd have to wait until Sunday to tell him her good news.

As she drove home, Charlie spied a market wagon coming from the opposite direction.

She recognized Nate in the driver's seat. She brightened. She wouldn't have to wait until Sunday after all.

As his vehicle approached, Charlie lifted her hand and waved to gain his attention. She pulled off the road, pleased when Nate parked his wagon and got out.

"Charlie," he said as he crossed the street. His expression flickered with concern. "Has something happened?"

"I went to your *haus*, saw your family. You must be happy to have them home."

He nodded. There was no sign of welcome in his expression. As she gazed at him, she felt a prickle of unease. "You need something from me?" he asked.

She swallowed hard. She wouldn't tell him her news. It was obvious that he wasn't pleased to see her. "I wanted to thank you for the birthday gift. I love the horse."

"I'm glad you like it," he said without feeling. He glanced back toward his wagon. "Anything else? I should get home. *Mam* is waiting for these groceries."

"*Nay*, you can go," she whispered as she held back tears. "I'll see you on Sunday."

"*Ja*, I'll see you then." Then he turned and crossed the street to his wagon, climbed in then left without another glance in her direction.

Hot tears escaped to dampen her face as she got into her buggy and continued home. Nate no longer needed her and didn't feel the need to be friendly toward her. She cried in earnest, her tears nearly blinding her as she drove home. How could he be so cruel?

She didn't understand this new, bewildering tension between them. Had her time with him during her birthday party been a dream? The laughter they'd shared while shopping together? Had she only imagined that he'd enjoyed her company? *And why did he go to the trouble of making me a special gift?*

Was it just something for him to do? She wiped away her tears so she could see. "A thank-you gift," she murmured, blinking rapidly. Nothing more. She shouldn't have hoped that it meant something more.

Nathaniel Peachy wanted to keep his distance from her, and she would accommodate him. She had a new job to look forward to. She'd be a good teacher and she'd enjoy her students while teaching them things they'd need for adulthood. And she would do her best to get over the heartache of her unrequited love for Nathaniel Peachy.

Nate clenched his jaw as he drove home. The image of Charlie's face when he'd fought to put distance between them would forever haunt him. He would miss seeing her every day, the light in her gorgeous green eyes when she was happy, the warm smile on her pretty pink lips when she was pleased. He had settled on his property recently, but having his own place meant nothing without a woman to share it with. This woman in particular, he realized. Charlie.

I love her. He could admit it to himself freely, but to no one else, most especially Charlie. The best thing he could do for her now was to nip their growing friendship in the bud.

If he hadn't known Emma, learned the truth of his failure and his inability to protect a loved one, he might have enjoyed a life with Charlie.

Tension clawed through him, causing his neck to tighten and his head to pound.

Jacob no longer needed her, but he did. Unlike him, she would get past the pain.

He was pleased that she liked his gift, but he couldn't show emotion. He couldn't allow her to see how special she was to him. If he did, his heart would crack open and spill the love he had for her inside.

He wanted her to be happy, and while he wanted to be the one to make her happy, to take care of her, protect her from the evils of the world, he knew better. Emma had taught him the truth about his failings.

Chapter Eleven

Charlie lay in bed and stared at the ceiling. She couldn't sleep, hadn't slept well in weeks. The excitement of securing the teaching position two weeks ago had been dimmed by the loss of her friendship with Nate. His lack of warmth when she'd encountered him on the road still bewildered her. His subsequent cool, unemotional behavior toward her ever since was like a harsh kick to her sensitive stomach, painful and making her gasp while unable to catch her breath.

She didn't understand him. She'd thought they'd stay friends after his family's return. She rubbed her aching temples with her fingers. Apparently, she'd been grossly mistaken about being Nathaniel Peachy's friend.

After tossing and turning as she tried to sleep, she finally gave up and got up. It was extremely early in the morning. The rest of her family would be in bed for hours yet. She felt anxious, antsy. Nate continued to weigh on her mind. She sought comfort with a visit to the horses, heading immediately to see her father's new gelding. As she stroked the animal's sleek neck, she felt the pinprick of tears. She still had the horse figure that Nate had carved for her. She couldn't get rid of it. It was the only thing she had that he'd given to her freely. Tears stung her eyes and she gasped out a sob.

It was a bitter cold December morning but she didn't care. She wanted to ride despite the weather. Charlie haltered Buddy then led him outside through the rear barn door. After shutting the door behind her, she swung up onto the horse's bare back and kicked his sides. Buddy sprang forward, and she cried out as she felt herself fly. The wind whipped through her hair, tearing at her prayer *kapp*, but she didn't care. The cold felt good against her face as she urged the horse into a gallop toward the back section of her father's farm. There was snow on the ground, but Buddy ran sure-footed, and she cried out with joy. For the first time in weeks, she was able to find happiness in something that wasn't Nate.

The gelding Buddy was young, and she

knew her father had paid good money for him. She'd ridden the family's horses before, but she'd been a child then. Now she was a woman who knew what she was doing, although her father might not be too pleased that she'd chosen Buddy to ride.

She hung tightly to the reins, laughing as she flew across farmland, her delight making her feel alive. Her prayer *kapp* loosened and she felt the pins give and her head covering fly off. Charlie reached to grab it, just as the gelding neared the road. She jerked on the reins the last minute to turn him back, and Buddy reared up, causing her to fall. She gasped with pain as she hit the ground. Filled with concern for her horse, she sat up, watching helplessly as Buddy ran off. She had to get him before he ran into the road and got hit by a car or worse. Her father would be angry with her when he found out. And once the elders learned of the incident, she'd lose the teaching position she'd wanted so desperately and then she'd have nothing.

Charlie closed her eyes. Maybe she hadn't changed at all. She struggled to her feet and looked down. Her stockings were torn but she wasn't hurt. But still she limped a little as she walked along the roadway while calling out for her runaway horse.

* * *

Nate drove his wagon along the road toward Adam Troyer's house. Adam had asked him to come early to help with a replacement window. It was barely dawn. Normally, they'd have tackled the work in the warmer weather, but the glass had been broken recently. And if the job wasn't done now, the cold winter weather would bluster inside the house, making it difficult to keep it heated.

Adam didn't expect him yet. It was too early, but Nate figured he'd take his time and head over. He had too much time on his hands—and too much on his mind—lately. And too many images of Charlie in his thoughts.

As if he'd conjured her from the air, he saw her. She was walking along the road that bordered the rear of her father's property. He scowled. Was she limping?

Nate parked his vehicle on the side of the road and rushed to her. "Charlie," he greeted with concern. "You hurt herself. What happened?"

He heard her groan with horror as she met his gaze. "I'm fine. I'm not hurt. And I'm not sure I want to tell you what happened."

Nate arched his eyebrow. "Tell me anyway."

"I took Buddy for a ride and fell off." Her

glistening eyes met his. "He bolted, and I have to find him. He's my *dat*'s newest gelding, and my *vadder* is not going to be happy that I've lost him."

He frowned. "'Tis slippery out here. There's snow on the ground. You could have been seriously hurt." He glanced down. "You were limping. Come with me."

She shook her head. "No need. I feel fine. And I'm not limping now. See?" She started to walk across the field. "I just want to find Buddy."

"Charlie!" He hurried up to her. "Are you sure you're *oll recht*?"

She gave him an annoyed look. "I'm fine."

"Then I'll help you look for him." He felt the hard thump of his heart as she looked up at him with bright green eyes. He accompanied her as she went right and crossed a field.

"If I don't find Buddy, I'll not only be in trouble with *Dat* but with the church elders, too. I'll lose my chances at being hired as teacher," she whispered brokenly.

He halted and reached for her hand. The sadness in her expression made him want to take her in his arms to comfort her. "We'll find Buddy," he promised, "and no one will know."

She stared at him. "You won't tell?"

He gave her a soft smile. "Tell what?"

Charlie rewarded him with a trembly smile. *"Danki."*

"But no more bareback riding, *ja*?" He caressed the back of her hand. "No more taking risks?"

She bit her lip and nodded. "Why are you being so nice? I didn't think you wanted to be my friend anymore."

Shocked, he released her hand. *"Charlie,"* he groaned. "'Tis not true."

"Except for Sunday, I haven't seen or talked with you in two weeks," she confessed. "And when we did see each other during church or Visiting Day, you avoided me. You barely acknowledged me. Like I didn't matter now that you no longer needed me for Jacob."

He closed his eyes for a long moment to control the yearning he felt for her. When he met her gaze, he shook his head. "'Tis not that, Charlie." He struggled to control his emotions. "I like you too much. 'Tis better that we don't get too close. The difference in our ages…"

"Pfft! You're the only one concerned with our age difference. I couldn't care less."

"Well, you should." He took off his hat and rubbed a hand across his forehead before he put it back on. "'Tis not only our ages. There are other reasons."

"What reasons?" There was an innocence in her features that made him want to forget about all the reasons why he shouldn't get involved with her.

"Charlie..."

She narrowed her gaze. "There are no reasons. You just don't like me."

"That's not true."

"Not like I want you to," she breathed and he stilled. "Nate, if those reasons, whatever they are, weren't there, then what? Would we be friends?"

He lifted his hand to run a finger along her cheek to her chin before he released her. "*Nay.* We'd have been more. I would have courted you and made you mine."

Joy burst inside her chest, making her heart speed up in response. Until he stepped back, and she saw his face. "Why can't we try? I like you, Nathaniel. More than any other man I know."

"Don't." He looked alarmed. "I'm not the right man for you."

Charlie saw something in his blue eyes that gave her courage. "I think you are."

He turned away, stared across the field. "Is

that the way Buddy went?" he asked, changing the subject.

"Nate, I want to talk more about this. Us."

"There is no us," he said sharply.

She drew back. "You won't consider it?"

"*Nay.* Now is that the way Buddy went?"

"Go away. I'll look for him myself."

"I'm not leaving until we find your horse and you and the animal are safely back inside."

"Fine!" she said with a huff. "*Ja,* he went that way." She gestured in the direction.

"We'd better hurry, then."

As if they'd spent too much time talking. Her lips firmed. "We should split up and search in different directions," Charlie suggested. She wanted to be alone. He'd hurt her feelings and she needed time to herself.

"I'm not leaving you alone," he said firmly. "We'll look together. Two sets of eyes are better than one."

"'Tis a horse," she replied drily. "Can't miss a chestnut gelding if he's within eye distance."

"Better still that I come along in case you need help catching him once you find him."

"More like you're afraid I'll hop on his back and ride off again," she muttered.

He stopped and caught her arm. "You promised. No more riding bareback."

She arched an eyebrow. "Did I?"

He didn't respond. His brow knitted as he gazed beyond her. She followed the direction of his gaze and gasped as he said, "There he is!"

To her relief, when she approached, Buddy didn't bolt. Nate remained several yards away. That he was allowing her to do the work when she suspected that he wanted to help made her love him more. Pain settled in her chest as she reached for Buddy's reins. She turned and caught him studying her with tenderness in his expression, which he quickly hid. Her resolve firmed. Somehow, someway, she'd convince Nate that the two of them belonged together. She didn't care about his reasoning for them to stay apart. She'd seen the look in his eyes, heard the regret and conviction in his tone when he'd told her that under different circumstances he would have courted her.

Brightening, she approached him with a smile and Buddy in tow. "I'll ride him back," she said cheekily, trying to get a rise.

His features became fierce. *"Nay, you won't."*

"I won't race him," she sweetly assured him.

"*Nay*, you won't. Because you won't be riding him back."

"Who's going to stop me?" She made as if to climb on.

He grabbed her by the waist with a growl. "You have to ask?"

Tenderness made her soften toward him. "I'll be fine, Nate. The only reason I fell was because I was trying to grab for my head covering."

"I'll be fine." She lovingly examined his features and saw genuine worry and fear. Charlie frowned.

"I can't let you ride back," he whispered emotionally. "I can't." He held out his hand. *"Please?"*

"You don't have to worry about me." But she gave him the leathers.

"As if I can breathe without worrying," he mumbled as he reached out to run a hand down Buddy's neck.

"Who will drive your buggy?" She knew she was pushing him but couldn't help herself. "You can't leave it here."

"You can," he said, surprising her. "I'll take Buddy and meet you behind the barn."

"And if my parents see you?"

He shrugged. "Buddy got away. I helped

you look for him." His smile was grim. "'Tis the truth."

She nodded. They wouldn't actually be lying. She didn't want to think about how wrong it was not to confess to her parents what she'd done. Charlie knew she'd tell them eventually. How could she not? She believed in right and wrong, and she'd always confessed the truth, even when it got her into trouble.

He started across the field toward the house. "Charlie," he called as she started to get into his vehicle. "Be careful."

Irritated, she wrinkled her nose. "I'll not damage your precious buggy, Nathaniel."

He changed directions and approached until he was close. He stared down at her with an exasperated expression. "You don't know me very well if you think it's the buggy I care about, Charlie." Then he tugged on a strand of her hair and walked away.

Her throat had gone dry. He'd told her that he cared for her. Hadn't he? She watched him start back across the field.

"Nate?" she called. He turned. *"Danki,"* she said, her voice soft as she gazed at him with affection. She glimpsed what looked like tenderness in his expression before he blinked and turned away.

Charlie was overwhelmed with a sense of satisfaction as she climbed into Nate's vehicle. She studied the interior of the vehicle. It smelled like him. A woolen hat lay on the seat next to her. A toolbox lay on the floor on the passenger side.

He liked her. Despite trying to, he'd been unable to hide it. Now she just had to figure out a way to fully break down his defenses and prove to him that they would be good together.

She didn't believe it was about age. It was something else that held him back. She flicked the leathers and steered the horse back to the house, where he'd be waiting for her. Nate was twenty-six. There must have been a girl in the past, someone he must have once cared about. Charlie fought a twinge of jealousy. Was that the main reason why he didn't want to get involved with her? Because of a girl in his past? Did he still love her?

After putting on the battery blinker, she made a turn. His concern for her, the look in his eyes when they'd talked, had any jealousy melting away. He cared about her. A lot. She was sure of it. And he'd already captured her heart.

He stood waiting for her by the barn when she pulled onto their dirt road. She left the vehicle close to the street. No sense raising her parents' awareness of Nate's presence and the reason he was here.

He didn't smile as she approached. She didn't care, as she suspected he was trying hard not to show any of his feelings. "Here in one piece, I see," he quipped.

She beamed at him. "I'm a capable driver—and rider," she added with a wink.

Nate laughed. "Come on. Let's put him in his stall."

She shot a look toward the house. "Why don't I take him? It might be better if you go before anyone sees you."

His good humor restored, he arched his eyebrow. "Ashamed of me?" he teased.

"Never," she said quietly, seriously.

The grin left his face as he handed her the leathers. "I'll leave. I promised to help Adam this morning."

"Danki," she murmured, her eyes locked with his. "I'll see you."

As he left, she followed him with her gaze and a deep-seated longing for him in her heart.

Chapter Twelve

Her first day at school had finally arrived. Elated, Charlie headed toward the Happiness schoolhouse on the edge of her aunt and uncle's property. It would be her first day as the new schoolteacher. She didn't feel as excited as she might have been. She missed Nate. Yes, she'd seen him on church Sunday, but that had been the only time, and he'd managed to avoid any time alone with her. She'd been hopeful of seeing him on Visiting Day, but the Abram Peachy family had been notably absent. At least to her.

How was she going to convince him that they belonged together if she never got to see or spend time with him?

The air was frigid. The wind whipped brutally through the morning against her legs as she climbed out of her buggy. As she let herself into the school, she found that someone had come earlier and thoughtfully fired up the woodstove. The classroom was warm and cozy. She ran back outside for the pine and holly she'd brought to decorate the classroom for Christmas. Her arms full, she struggled to get back inside. After setting the greenery on her desk, she took off her coat and hung it on the back of her chair. Then she spread pine and holly about the classroom, safely away from the heater.

Satisfied, Charlie took a good look at her surroundings, at the shelves flanking the front chalkboard, at the row of wooden desks, and the empty wall hooks just waiting for students' coats. She meandered about the room, recalling her days as a child. She'd loved school, and she hoped she could make every one of the children in her class love it, too.

Students talked and laughed as they filed into the school. She could feel their excitement with Christmas when they caught sight of the holiday greenery. One boy saw her in a corner and froze. Everyone grew quiet and stared at her.

"Hallo!" she greeted with a smile. "I'm Charlie Stoltzfus, your new teacher. As soon as you hang up your coats and get seated, we'll start."

"Did you bring us the holly and pine?" one little girl shyly asked.

"Ja." Charlie beamed at her. "I thought you'd enjoy a little holiday cheer."

"It looks nice!" another girl said.

"Ja," a young boy added. "'Tis nearly Christmas!"

The flurry of excitement over the holiday continued as she waited while the children hung up their coats then scrambled to their seats.

"Most of you already know me." She saw several heads bob. "But I think we should go around the room and say our names and a little about ourselves, don't you?"

She listened carefully to memorize names with the faces that she wasn't as familiar with, although she knew of most of her students' families.

"Josiah," she said to an older boy in the room after everyone had introduced themselves. "Has someone been assigned to hand out the readers?"

"I can do it," the boy offered.

"I'd appreciate that."

Charlie called on one of her younger students who was six years old. "Mary, can you tell me about the routine you had with Elizabeth?"

She listened carefully while the little girl

spoke, smiling at her as she explained about their morning and afternoon schedule. Sensing movement behind her, she glanced back and caught two boys exchanging secretive looks. She understood then that she might have a challenge on her hands with the two students.

The first part of the morning went quickly as the children changed desks to form smaller groups with an older student helping the younger ones with their English lesson. Afterward, Charlie taught weights and measures during their arithmetic session, then called a brief time-out for recess. Despite the cold, the children wanted to be outside. They bundled up warmly and went into the fenced play yard.

She had pulled on her own coat and bonnet and she stood outside the door watching her students interact. The younger children gravitated to the two swing sets while the older boys played baseball in an area away from the swings. A gathering of girls stood chatting and laughing as they watched the swing set. She smiled as one of the older girls broke away to check on a younger sibling and push her on the swing. The cold didn't seem to bother any of them.

She was infused with a sense of well-being.

She had enjoyed the morning, and her experiences teaching so far had been wonderful and fulfilling.

Charlie rang the handheld school bell. "Time to come in!" She observed as the children stopped what they were doing to return to the classroom. "If you're cold, warm yourself by the fire," she invited as they hung up their coats.

She recognized the glint of mischief in one boy's expression as he turned from the coat hooks and whispered something to a fellow student, who flashed her an uneasy glance.

"Thomas," she said, addressing the boy with a smile. "I understand you're good with multiplication. Do you think you could help Peter and James with it this afternoon?"

He shrugged and kept his gaze averted. Charlie let it go for now, but she would bring it up again this afternoon and insist that Thomas and the other boy, Ethan, be somehow engaged with their fellow students.

"Time for penmanship," she announced with a smile.

Nate had come to see how Charlie was making out on her first day as teacher.

Doing well, no doubt. He shouldn't be here, but he found he couldn't stay away. It had been weeks since he'd been close enough to talk with her. Although he was the one at fault, he still missed her. He longed to see her red hair, the bright green of her eyes and the way her lips curved whenever she smiled.

The play yard was empty as he parked his buggy some distance away on the dirt road that led to a cottage used by a number of teachers in the past. He didn't want her to see him. He didn't want to interrupt her work. He just needed a quick look inside. He took position near a window and peeked inside. A sudden gust of frigid wind buffeted him, and he shivered and hugged himself with his arms.

Charlie stood in the front of the classroom with her students seated in rows of desks facing her. Confident and in control, she was talking and gesturing with her hands. He experienced warm pleasure as he watched her movements, her bright smile that told him a student must have answered her correctly. She was in her element, and he couldn't be happier for her.

A sharper wind gust caught him off guard, slamming him against the side of the building. The noise drew her attention, and he groaned when her eyes widened in his direction. She said something to her students and disappeared from sight until the schoolhouse door opened. The air stilled as, bundled up in bonnet and cape, she exited and gazed at him warily.

"Nathaniel," she said. "What are you doing here?"

"I wanted to see you working on your first day." He gazed at her with amazement and pride at how naturally she'd handled her students.

She frowned. "Why?"

He closed his eyes. "To make sure you were *oll recht*." And he desperately needed to see her. It had been too long since he had.

"Seriously?" She became tight-lipped. "I'm teaching school, Nate, not riding bareback." Her features changed with her dismay. "You decided that I couldn't handle the job so you came to see if I needed help."

"That's not true!" His voice was loud in the stillness. It was as if God had ceased the wind for them to have this conversation.

"Isn't it?" she mocked. "Go away, Nate. I don't want you here." Her tone suggested that she didn't need him anywhere or anytime.

"I'll leave," he said softly. As he turned, the wind picked up, blowing against his bare head. He hugged himself tighter as he moved toward his buggy. He halted then spun back.

"Congratulations, Charlie. I know you're a great teacher."

She hadn't moved. Her features had softened with concern. "You're freezing, Nate. Come in out of the cold. You can warm up by the woodstove."

He debated whether to go or leave. He studied her expectant face and made his choice, then followed her inside.

"*Hallo*, Nate!" Several of the children chimed in to greet him.

He grinned at them, his face lighting up with pleasure. Charlie stared as more students called out to him. He was so good with children. Her heart gave a lurch and she felt a warm, fuzzy feeling inside.

"You come to join us?" one boy asked.

"Came inside to get warm. 'Tis freezing out. Just taking a moment by the woodstove." She saw how he noted all the rows of desks. "And I came to see Charlie."

"She your sweetheart?" an older boy asked with a smirk.

Charlie caught her breath as she waited for his answer.

He shot her a look as he took off his gloves and set them on the floor near the woodstove. "She could be, but right now she's a *gut* friend. A very *gut* one."

"You like her!" a little girl said.

"*Ja*, I do."

"Enough to come out in the cold to see her," the child added.

His lips curved. "Apparently." Charlie blushed as he caught and held her glance as if he was trying to send her a secret message. He had unbuttoned his coat to allow warmth to penetrate beneath. He rubbed his bare hands to warm them in the heat of the wood fire.

She swallowed hard as she became overwhelmed with confusion and love. His answers to the child's questions made her spirits rise. She turned to the class. "Children, let Nate get warm without all the questions. 'Tis time to get back to practicing your penmanship…"

Movement behind her caught her attention. She suffered extreme disappointment to see Nate buttoning his coat.

"I appreciate the use of your fire," he told her as he pulled on his gloves.

She eyed his bare head. "Why aren't you wearing a hat?"

"'Tis windy and I left it in the carriage."

"You should have worn a woolen cap," she murmured as she approached him.

"Ja, Mam," he teased with a twinkle in his blue eyes.

"You worry about me, but I can't worry about you?"

He sobered. "Charlie…"

Her pulse raced as she watched him. "What? What do you want from me?"

He broke eye contact. "I should go." After a smile for the children, he went to the door.

One of the students spoke up. "Nate?" When Nate looked at him in question, the boy said, *"Dat* said he saw you here early this morning. *Danki* for making it warm in here for us."

"You're *willkomm.*"

Charlie shot him a glance. He wouldn't look at her. "You fired up the stove?"

Nate reluctantly met her gaze. "It was nothing."

Her heart melted. Oblivious to her students, she placed a hand on his arm as he opened the door. "It wasn't nothing to me," she whispered with gratitude and love.

Then he left, and Charlie understood that something was changing between them. His kindness, his appearance, meant something more than a neighbor watching out for the new teacher. What it meant exactly, she wasn't sure.

Midweek came quickly. Charlie stood in the doorway of the school building and waved goodbye to her students as they left for the day. All in all, she'd had a great week with the highlight being Nate's visit two days ago. At first, she was hurt that he'd come, believing that he didn't trust that she would do a good job, that she'd help. But then his conversation with the children, learning that he'd come to the school early to make sure the classroom had warmed to a comfortable level, made her see his visit differently.

Every morning since, when she'd arrived, the school was toasty warm, and she knew it was because of Nate. She held on to hope. That he cared enough about her to go out of his way to come early to the school and fire up the stove made her believe that he had feelings for her that were more than just friendship. And after all, he'd told the children that she could be his sweetheart.

She longed to see him, but except for a brief stop before school started when she wasn't here, he didn't visit. She now slept better than she had in a long time because of Nate. She went back inside to prepare the building so that she could leave. She dampened the fire in the woodstove, put away pencils and any clean sheets of paper left on her students' desks, then bundled up against the cold in her black winter coat and traveling bonnet.

As she locked the door behind her, Charlie noticed an increased nip to the air. The sky was cloudy, and it looked like snow. She should take the time to stop and see her sister Meg's father-in-law. If anyone could accurately forecast the weather, it was Horseshoe Joe. After a severe injury to his leg while falling off a ladder years ago, he forecast the weather by the intensity of his pain.

Deciding to forgo the visit, she drove home. She was exhilarated by her success in the classroom but physically tired. She'd help *Mam* in the kitchen to prepare supper, then she'd seek an early bed. Christmas was only days away, and she'd be seeing Nate again. In light of their last encounter, she was delighted at the prospect. Life couldn't get much better than this, she thought with a smile.

With her first week of school over, Charlie had a brief pause. Saturday morning Charlie, her sister Ellie and her mother worked in the kitchen to put the finishing touches on a meal.

Nell, Leah and Meg were coming with their husbands. She was eager to see them, as she had much to tell them about her first week in school. After supper her family would head out to cut holly and pine boughs to decorate their houses for the upcoming holiday.

The morning had begun with snow flurries. With Horseshoe Joe, Peter's father and Meg's in-law, predicting a worsening of the weather, the family had decided to gather at midday instead of early evening.

Charlie grinned as Meg entered the house, her belly big with child. She gave her sister a hug then directed a smile at Peter. "Your *dat* still think there will be a heavy snow?"

"Ja," Meg answered with a smile at her husband. "And he's *gut* with his weather predictions."

Peter handed her a covered plate. "My dear Meg insisted we bring something," he said with a soft look toward his wife.

"'Tis your favorite dessert, husband. Are you complaining?" Her sister gazed at her husband with love.

"Never, wife. Never."

Charlie watched with longing in her heart for love like theirs—with Nate—as she followed them into the great room, where the rest of the family was gathered. Nell and

James sat close together in one corner of the room. Leah and Henry had taken a seat on a wooden love seat nearby. Her father and mother stood, happily chatting with the four of them. The genuine care and affection between her parents was apparent without a word or a touch.

The meal was a huge success. The topic of the Peachys' trip came up, and Charlie froze as the men discussed what they'd learned from Abram. When Nate's name entered the conversation in passing, she felt her face warm. She rose and started to clear the table. Her mother and sisters joined her, and the leftovers were put away and the dishes done in no time.

"Ready for holly and pine gathering?" Henry said with a smile.

"I ate too much." Meg groaned as she cradled her belly. "I'll just sit right here."

Peter bent close to her. "But, dearest wife, the exercise will be *gut* for you and our child."

Meg gave in graciously, and the family started to trek across their farm to a nearby woods just down the road.

"There!" Leah cried. "There's a holly tree!"

"I see pine," Nell exclaimed.

The family went to work, cutting holly and pine enough for each home. Every person carried an armful as they headed back to the house. Snow had begun to fall by then. Peter looked at the sky with misgiving. He was worried about Meg and suggested that they should leave. When the snow began to fall in earnest, everyone agreed. After storing their Christmas greenery in the backs of their vehicles, they left.

Charlie's mother gazed out the window with concern. "I'm glad they left," she said. "It doesn't look like it will be stopping anytime soon." Their holly and pine had been brought into the great room. Charlie and her sister Ellie grabbed several branches of pine and laid them on every available safe surface, well away from the heater.

Charlie felt the loss of her married sisters' company. Two hours later she, too, was glad they'd left. It was a blizzard outside with heavy snowfall and the sudden fierce onset of wind, which blew in every direction. She could barely see outside.

There was only one weekday before Christmas, and that was Christmas Eve. Fortunately, they didn't have to worry about getting to school in the inclement weather. School wasn't scheduled to resume until after second Christmas, which was the day after Christmas and five days away. The increasing intensity of this snowstorm was frightening. The only need to venture outdoors was to take care of the animals that were safely in the barn.

Her mother and father relaxed in the great room. Ellie was upstairs in her bedroom. Charlie turned from the window and decided to work on her lesson plans in her room.

"Heading upstairs," she told them.

"Going to work on your lesson plans?" her mother asked.

"*Ja*, I brought some books home with me. I thought I'd go over them and come up with a lesson plan to make learning more fun."

"You enjoy teaching," her father said.

Charlie smiled. "I love working with children."

"Someday you'll have children of your own," he said.

She murmured an answer then left them. As she climbed the stairs to the second story, she thought of Nate and her desire to wed and have children with him. Once in her room, lesson plans were the last thing on her mind as she was consumed by thoughts of Nate. The thought that she might never have his love brought tears to her eyes and an increasing ache in her heart. She wasn't about to give up on him. She straightened and opened a schoolbook. Her gaze skimmed the page's contents, then she looked up with a sigh.

I would have courted you and made you mine. His words came back to her in a flash and her heart lightened. Their age difference meant nothing. His reasons, although she didn't know what they were, meant nothing. She would just have to talk with him to convince him.

She grinned. *"I need you, Nathaniel Peachy,"* she murmured. "I won't settle for less."

Chapter Thirteen

Sunday morning the snow stopped abruptly. The plows came through early afternoon, making it easier for her church community members to handle any necessary outside farm chores. Church had been canceled that morning, but her family had gathered to pray.

The sun cast a glow into her room, drawing Charlie to the window. She stared outside, noting the thick snow covering the yard. Her cousin Isaac had stopped by, not long after the roads had been plowed. He'd driven over in a sleigh to let them know that the roads were good and the church elders had decided that there should be school on Christmas Eve. School would be closed for Christmas and Second Christmas before resuming on Thursday, the next day.

The temperature dropped by the next

morning, keeping a layer of packed snow on the streets. Word about school had traveled, thanks to her Lapp cousins. Elijah had arranged those for whom he'd crafted sleighs to transport students safely to the schoolhouse. Her cousin Isaac would be coming for her.

She dressed quickly in winter gear after she saw a sleigh pull into the yard. Isaac was bundled up with his heavy dark coat and a navy woolen hat. Charlie made sure every inch except her face was covered. "I'm leaving for *schuul*!" she called to her mother from the bottom of the stairs. "Isaac's here!"

Her mother appeared at the top. "Say *hallo* to him. Will he be bringing you home?"

She grinned. "One of my cousins will."

Her *mam* smiled. "Have a *gut* day, Charlie, and be careful. 'Tis icy out there."

"I will, *Mam*." Then she left by the back and shrank back against the cold wind that whipped inside, bringing an instant chill into the kitchen.

Head down, she ran toward the sleigh. She didn't look up but felt a presence and grabbed the hand that appeared in front of her. She gasped as he caught her by the waist and lifted her easily onto the seat. She tugged her coat against the cold as she waited for Isaac to climb onto the other side.

"Here," a deep, familiar voice that was not her cousin's said as he wrapped a blanket around her.

"Nate," she gasped. "I didn't expect you."

He gave her a wry smile. "Isaac said you needed a ride."

Blinking against the wind, she studied him. "And so you got unlucky?" Had he offered to take her or had he been roped in? If he'd wanted to see her, he could have come to see her sooner at school.

He stared at her. "Don't be silly—"

"I'm going to be late." She pulled the blanket around her more tightly.

Nate didn't immediately move. She refused to look at him, and he finally flicked the leathers. She didn't speak as he steered the horse-drawn sleigh toward the schoolhouse. She didn't know what to say, because she knew she'd overreacted. It was good to see him, and she'd been unable to tell if he felt the same way. Fearing the worst, she'd acted badly.

She knew she should apologize, but the wind made conversation difficult. With him so near, she was conscious of his every move. He had seen to her comfort and stirred up feelings she wanted to share with him but was afraid to.

Tears filled her eyes and the wind blew them across her skin, dampening her temples and her cheeks. The schoolyard loomed ahead, and Charlie realized that she probably wouldn't see him this afternoon. Nate parked the sleigh close to the school.

"Danki," she said and turned to flee.

He caught her arm. "Charlie."

She froze. She started to tremble as she met his gaze. "It was nice of you to come to bring me."

"I wanted to bring you. I *volunteered* to get you."

She blinked. "You did?"

"Ja." He leaned in close. "Don't move. I want to help you get down." There was warmth in his gaze but his tone brooked no argument.

Nate skirted the sleigh to get to Charlie's side. Then he followed her to the building and waited as she tried using the key to unlock the door. He noted that her fingers shook too much to insert the key. He gently took it from her and quickly unlocked the door. She looked half-frozen but she didn't complain.

"Danki," she murmured after he'd opened the door and gestured her in. "I know you have to go."

"I have a minute," he said as he went to build a fire in the woodstove. Shivering, Charlie hugged herself with her arms and watched him, but didn't say a word. Confident that the fire would take, he faced her. "It won't take long to get warm."

She blinked rapidly and that was when he noticed that her eyes seemed overly bright. He gave a sound of sympathy when he saw the frozen tear tracks on her cheeks. "You're always taking care of me," she whispered.

Nate gave her a tender smile. "I don't mind." It wasn't hard to give her help when she needed it. He surveyed the classroom, taking more time to note the large letters near the ceiling around the perimeter of the room, the room full of desks…the teacher's desk in the front right corner.

"What time do you normally start?" he asked. It had been a long time since he'd been in school, and he wasn't sure if the schedule had changed in the ensuing years.

"In about a half hour." She paused. "But I don't expect everyone to be on time this morning."

"I should go…" He felt a tightness in his chest. He didn't want to leave her, but there were children waiting for him. He watched as Charlie shifted closer to the stove and held out her hands to warm them. "I need to pick up your students. Will you be *oll recht* here alone?"

"I'll be fine," she assured him. She met his gaze, her green eyes glistening. "I appreciate the ride."

"It was my pleasure." In fact, if he hadn't been told to get her, he would have insisted. It had been too long since he'd spent any time with her.

Nate gazed at her a long moment as the wind rattled the windows and gusted against the sides of the building. "I'll see you later," he said as he turned toward the door.

"Nate!" she called and he stopped in his tracks. She approached. "Can we talk later?"

He shifted uncomfortably. As much as he wanted to spend time with her, he didn't think it was wise.

He must have taken too long to answer. "Never mind," she said.

The wind buffeted him as he climbed onto his sleigh. He took one last long look at the building and caught sight of Charlie in the window watching him. He stifled the feelings growing within his chest and headed toward the road. The house behind the school was vacant. The last teacher hadn't lived there during her time as schoolteacher. If the winter continued like this for the rest of the winter, it might be best if Charlie stayed at the cottage so that she wouldn't have to worry about the snow.

The cold bit into his cheeks and he reached up to pull his woolen hat over his ears. He didn't like the thought of her living alone even in the cottage, even though it wasn't far to her aunt and uncle's place. She would be alone.

She wanted to talk. He closed his eyes briefly before he got onto the sleigh. They probably should talk. But what would he say that wouldn't be a lie? If she asked, he couldn't tell her that he didn't care, because he did care for her. He loved her.

He had to remember Emma. If he didn't, he'd give in to his feelings for Charlie, and then he'd fail her, too.

Charlie watched as her students straggled in after they were dropped off by sleigh at school. Thanks to Nate, the room was toasty and warm. The children murmured with relief as they took off their coats and hung them up. The children chatted happily. It didn't seem to bother them that they were in school the day before Christmas.

The school day ended quickly, and sleighs arrived to bring the children home. She smiled and waved as they left. She caught sight of Nate helping students onto his sleigh. She waited for him to acknowledge her but he never did. He left and she turned back inside to wait for her ride.

She was more than ready to go home. She didn't understand why the elders decided that there should have been school today, unless they knew something that she didn't. Like another blizzard was on its way. She pulled on her coat and put on her traveling bonnet while she waited. A half hour passed and then an hour. She became worried when no one came. She hadn't fed the fire since she was due to leave, and it was already getting cold inside. Where was Isaac?

Snow fell heavier than before. If she didn't get home soon, she'd be stuck in the schoolhouse. There was a little firewood left but not enough to keep her warm all night.

Then she remembered the teacher's cottage close by. Wasn't it heated with wood or propane? She didn't know. And besides, how would she get inside if she needed to? It wasn't as if someone had given her a key.

The howl of wind against the roof made her shiver. She searched for a key in her desk and panicked when she couldn't find one. Should she rebuild the fire? Venture outside to bring in more wood? Any wood there would be snow-covered and probably too wet to burn. She hugged herself with her arms and tried not to cry. She had to think clearly, to decide what to do.

There was a loud pounding on the door. Relieved, she hurried to answer it. Her ride was finally here. She swung open the door and stared.

"Nate!" Relief and joy hit her hard. She felt suddenly safe, and although she was freezing, she felt a burst of warmth that sprang from her heart.

He brushed past her as he entered, his jacket and hat covered in snow. "You're still here," he said as if stunned. "Why are you still here?"

"No one came for me," she replied, her voice wobbly. She bit her lip. "You didn't know?"

"*Nay*, I just stopped to make sure everyone was gone. I never expected anyone to be here." She shivered, and Nate gazed at her with an intensity she found disconcerting. He made a sound of concern. "You're freezing." He started to unbutton his coat.

"*Nay*, I don't want to take your coat. You'll

get sick." Charlie placed her fingers over his to stop him. "I'm fine." Now that he was there.

"Are you sure?" He continued to eye her worriedly.

She bobbed her head. "*Ja*, I'm sure." He stole her breath when he reached out and rubbed her arms with his gloved hands.

"I'll be right back," he said. He locked gazes with her. "I promise." Then he opened the door and disappeared into the white.

She grew colder after he left her. Fortunately, he was back within seconds with a dry quilt wrapped in plastic in his arms. "I had this under the seat." He tugged off the plastic before he unfolded the quilt and placed it around her shoulders until she was cocooned with warmth. His eyes held emotion as he studied her. "You've got your key?"

"*Ja.*"

"Let's go, then." Placing his arm around her, he held her against him as they left the building. "'Tis bad out," he murmured close to her ear. "Keep your head down." She felt the heat of him as he steered her through the storm to his sleigh. After making sure she was still wrapped up in the quilt, he stepped up onto the side of the sleigh and set her gently onto the seat.

"You *oll recht*?" He observed her without moving.

"I'm fine." She blinked rapidly. "*Danki*, Nathaniel."

His tender concern brought her to the verge of tears. She desperately wanted this man in her life, and if she didn't figure a way to get him soon, she'd be destined to be unhappy forever.

Apparently reassured, Nate skirted the vehicle and climbed onto the driver's side. The wind continued to blow snow, hampering visibility, but Charlie wasn't worried. She was with Nate and she knew he wouldn't let anything bad happen to her.

No one had come to pick up Charlie. The knowledge upset him. He'd been assured by her cousins that one of them would be bringing her home. He would have come sooner if he'd known. Nate wasn't sure why he felt the need to stop at the school and double-check. He thanked the Lord that he had. Seeing Charlie teary-eyed, cold and scared had him yearning to take her in his arms and hold on tight.

As he steered the horse through the snow toward the Arlin Stoltzfus residence, he experienced the strongest desire to take her home where he could take care of her, ensure she was safe and warm. The wind, strong at first, died down, and the snow fell softly over the sleigh and the landscape. He shot her a glance. She sat, wrapped in a blanket, her eyes ahead. "Charlie." She looked at him. "You'll be home in a few minutes," he said.

She nodded. "*Danki*. I don't know what I would have done if you didn't come when you did."

The thought of what might have happened terrified him. He kept his gaze on the road as he fought his fear. "I should have come for you sooner, but I thought Isaac or Elijah had taken you home."

"But yet you stopped to make sure." Her voice was soft, almost affectionate.

He met her gaze briefly before returning his attention back to the road. "*Ja...*" He couldn't finish. How could he admit that he'd worried about her, that he always worried about her? She was constantly in his thoughts. She wasn't Emma, because she wasn't a child. His feelings for her were different than the ones he'd felt for Emma.

They were silent for the rest of the ride. Nate checked for oncoming traffic before he steered the sleigh onto the road on her father's property. He parked close to the porch steps, climbed down and ran around the vehicle before Charlie had a chance to move. She turned and he reached up and lifted her out, setting her down in front of him. Close, they gazed at each other for several long moments. He noticed the vivid green of her eyes, her cheeks pink from the wind and her perfectly formed mouth. His hand lifted on its own, touched her skin reddened from the cold.

"Nate…"

"You should get inside. You're freezing."

She inclined her head. "Come in for a minute for something hot to drink? You can have coffee, tea or hot chocolate."

He shouldn't. He should probably go, but he couldn't resist her. "A quick minute." The way her eyes brightened made his heart pump harder.

Her smile was soft as she lifted her gloved hand to stroke his cheek. "As much as you've rescued me, you probably think I need a keeper," she murmured.

His chest tightened. *"Ja,"* he whispered.

"Maybe I do. And I wouldn't mind one if it were you." She turned and hurried up the steps, her words leaving him shocked and standing still. She flashed a concerned look over her shoulder. "Nate? Aren't you coming?"

Stunned, he followed her up the stairs. He took off his woolen cap before entering the house.

"Mam! Dat!" she called out. "I'm home!"

"Praise the Lord," her mother said, her brow clearing as she exited the kitchen. "I was worried. 'Tis late—" She stopped. "Nathaniel! What a nice surprise."

"Nate gave me a ride. He's been transporting students all afternoon. I think he could use something to warm him." She smiled at him. "How about a mug of hot chocolate?"

"Sounds *gut*." He'd answered automatically. Charlie's words kept playing silently in his mind.

Before he gave it another thought, she grabbed his hat. "Take off your coat," she urged. He took off his coat, and she grabbed it and headed into the kitchen. He followed her, immediately feeling the warm coziness of the room. When her mother followed them in, he felt the kitchen fill with love.

Charlie opened the door then held out his coat to brush off the snow. When she was done, she hung it up then handed his hat to her *mam*.

Missy disappeared into a back room while Charlie retrieved milk from the refrigerator and a pot out of a kitchen cabinet. She poured a generous helping of milk into the pot, then turned on the stove. Nate watched her as she moved about the kitchen. He was comfortable in the Stoltzfus kitchen, comfortable with Charlie. He almost could imagine her living in another house, the small farmhouse he'd finally managed to purchase recently, cooking on his stove. *As his wife.*

Charlie added rich chocolate to a mug of milk. "Whipped cream?" He shook his head. With a smile, she set it down before him. "Here you go." She smiled at him. "Want some cookies? We have chocolate chip."

"*Ja*, that sounds *gut*." He couldn't keep his eyes off her. Surprisingly, the image of her in his life was crystal clear and not unwelcome.

She flashed him a pleased look before she put several cookies on a plate. He eyed the treats as she placed them on the table. "Help yourself." He could feel her gaze on him as he took two cookies. He glanced up.

She smiled at her mother as Missy entered the room. Missy handed something to her daughter. Charlie turned and extended a dry knit cap toward him. "This is *Dat*'s. He has plenty to lend. Nate, please take this. I'll give you back yours, but 'tis too wet for you again."

Nate accepted the woolen hat. "I'll return it," he promised.

She nodded then made herself a mug of hot chocolate and sat across from him.

He wanted desperately to continue the conversation they'd started outside. About her needing a keeper and her wanting it to be him. But it was neither the time nor the place for it. And it wasn't something he'd want to discuss in front of her mother.

"I'm glad you could stay for a while," she said softly.

"You are?"

"*Ja.* I…" She suddenly blushed and looked away. She stood abruptly, as if she was suddenly uncomfortable and couldn't sit still.

Charlie was pretty and smart, and she had a sense of humor. He loved looking at her. And he loved who she was. He wouldn't want to change her. He cared about her, felt the ever-present need to protect her. *To love her.*

He left shortly afterward with her father's hat on his head, a full belly and a warm heart. And with thoughts of Charlie.

He had to talk with her. He now understood that no matter how hard he tried he wasn't going to stop loving her. But their discussion would have to come later. At present, it would take all of his concentration to drive home as the increasing snowstorm became a blizzard that threatened his and his horse's safety.

Chapter Fourteen

Charlie worried about Nate as she watched him leave. It was a blizzard outside and he had a long way to get home. She was confident in his abilities to drive the sleigh, but she couldn't help but fear the storm. She loved him. Worrying and caring went hand in hand with love. She stood on the front porch until his sleigh disappeared from sight, which wasn't long given the whiteout conditions. She offered a silent prayer for his safety. Her mother would need help with the meal. She needed to keep busy or go crazy with thoughts of Nate in an accident.

"Is Ellie home?" she asked as she entered the kitchen. She looked forward to working in the kitchen with her mother and sister as they prepared supper together.

Mam nodded. "She heard the weather forecast and came home before noon."

Charlie thanked God. Her sister was safe and she needed to have faith that soon Nate would be safe, too. "I'll call her downstairs."

"That was nice of Nate to bring you home," *Mam* commented while she put the water on to boil potatoes as Charlie reentered the room.

"Ja." She picked up a potato peeler and began to take the skin off a potato. "I'm not sure what I would have done if he hadn't stopped to make sure everyone had gone safely home."

"You were all alone?" Ellie asked sharply, having overheard the conversation as she entered.

"Ja, and I was getting cold. I didn't stoke up the fire since we were leaving and there's no school tomorrow. I thought Isaac or Elijah was coming to get me. Nate was upset to learn that I'd been left behind."

"Thank the Lord that he came back for you." Her mother pulled bread out of a cabinet and set it on a cutting board.

Charlie murmured her agreement. Nate had rescued her. *Again.* She was always happy to see him, but this afternoon her fear of being abandoned in a cold building had gotten the best of her. She'd wanted to rush into his arms and hug him hard. Feel his strength surround her. He always made her feel warm and protected.

She recalled the times she'd rebelled when someone—Nate—had wanted to help her or warned her to be careful. She'd once thought relying on help meant she couldn't be independent. But the more she learned about herself—and Nate, the more she considered things differently. She'd come to know about the man's character. His kindness and concern were an integral part of him. And she loved him for exactly who he was.

Before he'd left for home, she'd caught him studying her intently, and it wasn't dismissal she'd seen in his gaze. And not just concern for her well-being. There had also been affection and a hint of longing in his striking blue eyes.

Please, Lord, please bless a union between us. They needed to talk. And she'd recognized that he wanted to talk as much as she did.

With the blizzard currently roaring across the countryside, it could be days before she saw him again. Days she could be cooped up inside the house with him constantly on her mind.

There was nothing she could do about it,

but hope and pray that the Lord would decide that Nate and she belonged together.

"Christmas is tomorrow," *Mam* commented as she kneaded dough for flat dumplings.

"I'm ready," Charlie said. "What if the snow doesn't let up?"

Ellie started to slice the bread. "We'll have to make do."

"The snow will make for a white Christmas." *Mam* flattened the dough with a rolling pin.

"I don't mind a little snow, but while I love spending the holiday with you, *Mam*, and Ellie—and *Dat*—I really want to see Nell and James, Meg and Peter, and Leah and Henry." *And Nate.* She really wanted to see and talk with Nate. She had a special gift to give him and she couldn't wait to see his reaction. It wasn't as nice as the horse he'd given her for her birthday, but she had put a lot of thought into her present for him. She hoped he liked it.

"Something smells *gut*," her father said with a smile as he entered the kitchen.

"Where were you?" Ellie asked.

"Upstairs changing into dry clothes. I fed the animals." He viewed the women in the kitchen with affection.

"We haven't started to cook yet," *Mam* teased.

"Then why do I smell cake?" *Dat* grinned. He looked at the kitchen worktable. "You're making dumplings..."

"*Ja*, I know it's unusual to have potatoes and dumplings at the meal."

He grinned. "You'll not hear any complaints from me. I love both."

Charlie looked from her father to her mother and back. This was what she wanted—a loving relationship and marriage like her parents had. And the only one she could see herself married to was Nathaniel Peachy. *Please, Lord, please let him love me.*

Nate couldn't get Charlie out of his mind. Ever since he'd found her nearly freezing in the schoolhouse, he'd been consumed with thoughts of her.

He wanted to see her, needed to spend time with her. The snow had finally tapered off, and everyone was waiting for the roads to be plowed again. If the streets weren't cleared soon, then he'd walk to the Arlin Stoltzfus farm. It wouldn't be a Christmas celebration without Charlie. And it was well past the time to tell her of his feelings. And to find out if she returned them.

He loved her. The realization had come over him slowly, and he almost hadn't recognized it until he found her alone and half-frozen in the school. Charlie wasn't Emma, and he was older and wiser now. If the Lord gave him a second chance, he wouldn't fail.

Charlie wasn't foolish. She was industrious, kind and loving. Yet she'd teased and taunted him until he'd seen only red. He saw some of the things she did as dangerous, but she wasn't a child and she could handle herself.

Warmth settled in his chest as he thought about the possibility of having a life with her. Nate smiled. He still had to fix up the farmhouse he'd bought before they could move in, but he was certain Charlie would be pleased to live there after he was done renovating it.

He imagined Charlie holding his baby, caring for him, loving him. He grinned. The image was as clear as his view of the snow outside.

In a few hours it would be Christmas. He was eager to give Charlie her gift. If her reaction to her birthday gift was any indication, then she would love what he'd made for her.

The roar of a truck engine and the scrape of metal against snow drew him to open the side door. A huge snowplow cut a huge swath over the snowy street. He grinned. He'd be spending Christmas with Charlie.

On Christmas Day, Nate waited until afternoon when his family had exchanged gifts and enjoyed a big breakfast. Eager to see Charlie, he told his parents he was going out. Bundled up in warm, dry clothing, he went outside to prepare the sleigh. With no real plan in mind, he drove away from the house and steered his horse toward Charlie's.

The snow shimmered under the sun, which brightened the landscape. He drove past a farm where horses had been released inside a fence. The wind had blown snow, leaving an uncovered section of the paddock. The animals frolicked about the enclosure as if overjoyed to have the freedom of outdoors after being cooped up inside their dark stalls.

Nate slowed the sleigh and watched them. He knew instinctively that Charlie would love seeing them. Maybe he could convince her to take a ride with him and he could show her.

He turned onto the road leading to the Arlin Stoltzfus house. The horse-drawn sleigh glided along without a sound as he parked. He got out and tied up the horses on a fence post near the barn. His heart started to race as he went to the front door. His breath quickened, and he could see the vapor it emitted into the chilly air each time he exhaled. He rapped on the door and waited.

Suddenly, the door opened. Nate stared then smiled as he faced the woman he loved. He was encouraged when her green eyes widened with pleasure and her pretty pink lips curved into a wondrous smile. She wore a green dress that deepened the vibrant color of her eyes. She gazed at him without a word. He didn't worry, for she looked stunned but happy to see him.

"May I come in?" he asked with genuine amusement.

"*Ja! Ja,* of course!" She stepped back to allow him entry. "The roads are *gut*?"

"*Ja.*" He continued to study her. His gaze caressed her features, enjoying what it saw.

She frowned. Clearly, she hadn't expected to see him until tomorrow, Second Christmas, the day for visiting. "Is everyone well? Your *mam*—is it the baby?"

"*Nay,* she's not due until after Christmas," he said. "She's fine."

Charlie released a sharp breath. "*Gut,* that's *gut.*" She smiled and her eyes softened. "Although a Christmas baby would be truly blessed."

Watching her, picturing her in his mind again as his wife with a baby in her arms and a loving smile on her face, startled him. "*Ja,* it would," he agreed gruffly.

"Why are you here?" Her beautiful green eyes gazed at him warily.

"Would you like to take a ride? There's an English farm not far from here, and the farmer let out his horses."

She blinked rapidly as if suddenly overcome with emotion. "You want me to see horses with you?"

He inclined his head. "'Tis chilly outside so you will need a warm coat and hat if you come." He swallowed hard. "Do you want to?"

She bobbed her head. "*Ja*, that would be *wunderbor*." She turned. "Just let me get my coat."

"Charlie." Nate softened his expression as he approached her. He reached out to tenderly stroke her cheek. He heard her sharp intake of breath and quickly withdrew. "Don't forget your hat, too."

"Okay."

"Oh, and Charlie?" he called out, stopping her again. "Merry Christmas," he said softly.

Charlie grinned. "Merry Christmas, Nate." She was happy and excited as she invited him to follow her as she went to the kitchen to get her winter garments. He had come to visit her on Christmas Day, as if he couldn't wait one more day to spend time with her. And he wanted to take her to see the horses! He knew how much she loved the animals, and he wanted to share what he'd seen. Her parents were at the table when she and Nate entered the room.

"Nathaniel," her mother greeted. "'Tis nice to see you. Merry Christmas."

"Merry Christmas, Missy. Arlin." He gave each one a respectful nod.

"Did you have trouble with the roads?"

"*Nay*, Missy. The sleigh glides easily over the packed snow."

Arlin frowned as his daughter put on her coat. "Going out?"

"I've invited Charlie on a sleigh ride. There are some horses I think she'll enjoy seeing."

Missy smiled. "She loves horses. She'll enjoy them, I'm sure."

"*Ja*, I will," Charlie agreed. Her gaze settled on her father, who studied Nate thoughtfully. She hoped and prayed that *Dat* didn't say anything to embarrass her.

"You'd better dress warm, *dochter*," *Dat* instructed.

Nate grinned. "That's what I said."

Her father looked at him approvingly. "How are your *eldre*?"

"Doing well. We all are. Jacob is fully recovered from his accident with the mower."

The conversation was nice, but Charlie was eager to spend time with Nate. She grabbed her coat from a hook and suddenly it was taken out of her hands. Nate smiled down at her as he held it open for her. She tingled with pleasure as she placed an arm into each sleeve. She saw something shift in her *dat*'s expression as he watched Nate's courteous act. She swallowed hard as she wondered what her father was thinking.

"I'm ready," she said, stating the obvious.

"Will you be gone long?" her *dat* asked.

"About an hour at the most. 'Tis too cold for Charlie to spend more time outside."

Her father nodded.

"Don't forget to tie your bonnet strings," Nate said gently. Charlie frowned at him. She didn't like him being bossy while her parents looked on. But when she looked at her father and saw his approval, she relaxed and secured her bonnet.

"I'll make a pot of coffee for when you come back," her mother said.

"Sounds *gut*," Nate replied with a smile.

Charlie headed toward the front door, eager to be away from her parents' prying eyes. She extended her hand toward the doorknob but

Nate reached over her shoulder to open the door for her.

She was all set to object until the brightness of the day calmed her. "'Tis so nice to see the sun." She wanted Nate's attention. Why fight it when she had exactly what she'd desired?

Nate was quiet as they reached his sleigh. When she glanced up, he was smiling down at her.

"What?" she whispered. "Why are you looking at me like that?" Although she loved seeing good humor in his eyes.

"I like seeing you happy."

Her breath caught. *You make me happy*, she longed to say but didn't. "I am happy," she said and his eyes flared. "'Tis nice to be outside without a blizzard."

Nate surrounded her waist with his hands and lifted her onto the seat. He quickly released her then climbed onto the other side. "Are you warm enough?"

Charlie watched his breath release as warm mist into the frigid air. She felt her insides melt as she gazed into his beautiful blue eyes. "I'm fine."

He reached for something under the sleigh seat. "I brought this just in case." He pulled out the quilt he'd wrapped her in when he'd picked her up from the school yesterday and handed it to her.

"'Tis dry." She smiled at him as she unfolded it. "I think we should share it," she said as she laid it across both of their laps.

He didn't move to grab the reins. He studied her silently, intently, for several long seconds with a look that made her toes curl and her heart skitter within her chest. "Ready to go, then?"

"I'm ready." He flicked the leathers and she grabbed the edge of her seat as the horse moved forward.

Snow sparkled on tree branches, house roofs and lawns. Charlie felt a sense of inner peace and well-being as she took in her surroundings. She only felt this way in Nate's company, she realized. Everything looked better and richer with Nate next to her.

It wasn't long before Nate pulled the sleigh to the side of the road and gestured toward the pasture. "There."

She looked and inhaled with wonder. "They're beautiful!"

The three horses within the paddock were all chestnut brown. They looked healthy and well cared for with their shiny coats and strong bodies. They pranced and ran in circles, chasing each other. Charlie laughed with delight. Nate was silent beside her, but his lips curved when she flashed him a grin. *"Danki."*

"Would you like get a closer look?" he asked with good humor.

Charlie studied the snowy ground and the pile made by the snowplow along the edge of the roadway. She didn't think it would be wise to stay parked there. And she didn't relish the thought of stepping knee-deep into icy snow.

"I can see well enough from here." She was happy enough to enjoy the view from here, on the seat right next to Nate. They could stay a moment then move on if a car came.

He was silent. She turned to find him studying the scenery with a thoughtful look. As if sensing her regard, he met her gaze. "Your cheeks are pink," he commented huskily.

"Oh!" She held her gloved hands up to her face. "I must look silly."

"Nay. You look beautiful," he said with a serious look in his eyes. He took her hands from her face and replaced them with his gloved fingers. He cupped her cheeks as he gazed into her eyes and then stared at her mouth. "Are you feeling warmer?"

She bobbed her head.

"I don't remember seeing you speechless before," he said. He pulled off a glove and stroked her face with warm fingers. "Do I make you nervous?"

She held his gaze, shook her head. *"Nay,"* she whispered. "You make me feel other things."

His blue gaze sharpened. "Things?"

"Ja, gut things."

He released her but held her attention. "Charlie—what you said…"

"About?"

"Me…" He stopped, looked away, almost as if afraid of her reply. "Us."

"About you being my keeper?" she finished for him quietly as she regarded him with tenderness.

He locked gazes with her. *"Ja."*

"You don't want to be?" She softened her expression. "I'd like you to be."

"And who is a keeper to you?"

"He is someone, like you, who is there for me when I need him. Someone who wants to protect and care for me. Someone I'll love forever and who loves me back." She briefly closed her eyes. "A husband to me and father to my children." She swallowed as she gazed at him. She couldn't read him. "That's what a keeper means to me." There was emotion in his expression, but she couldn't get a read on it.

"And you," he began in a strangled voice, "want me?"

She smiled and reached up to grab his bare hand. "You're a *gut* man, Nathaniel Peachy. I've never met or known anyone better. I know I'm not the sort of person you envisioned for your sweetheart. I tend to be independent and I like to do things on my own… I'm impulsive and prone to getting into trouble."

He tugged on her hand to pull her against him. "You may be exactly what I need, Charlie Stoltzfus."

She beamed at him. *"Ja?"*

He cupped her face, then kissed her gently before placing her back in her seat. "Have you seen enough of the horses for today? Your *vadder* will be wondering where we are. I don't want to make him angry after our first outing."

"First?" she breathed.

"Ja, first," he said. "And there will be more." She saw something in his eyes that made her sigh with pleasure. "I'd like to court you, Charlie Stoltzfus, the proper way. Will you let me?"

She felt warmed by the sun and the man. *"Ja,* I'd very much like that."

He grinned at her as he ran fingers down her cheek briefly then let her go. "*Gut*. Let me take you home."

Chapter Fifteen

Second Christmas Day dawned bright and clear. Charlie had hidden her Christmas gift for Nate under her bed. Besides her sisters with their husbands, Nate and his family were coming for dinner, as were all of her Lapp relatives. Yesterday Nell, Meg and Leah had helped to make extra food. Ellie and she had worked hard to clean the house yesterday after Nate had brought her home from their ride.

The scent of pine filled the air. The snow that blanketed the lawn made for another glorious and blessed holiday. She still couldn't believe that Nate wanted to court her. It was her dream come true and her best Christmas gift ever.

The first of their visitors began to arrive at nine thirty. Aunt Katie and Uncle Samuel came with Daniel, Joseph and Hannah, their three children who lived with them. Charlie's married sisters were due to arrive shortly after them. Soon everyone was there but the Peachy family, and the house felt near to bursting at the seams with people intent on having a good time. One hour passed and then another. She went to the window several times. The morning had grown late and yet Nate and his family hadn't come.

Had he changed his mind about courting? Maybe he didn't want to let her down in front of her family and friends. She quickly dismissed the feeling. Nate loved her, she was sure. Something else must have happened to make them late. But what? Concern filled her as she recalled that Charlotte Peachy's baby was due in just a few short weeks. Had she gone into labor? What if something worse had happened? Like the family had suffered an accident while on their way over?

She had to go to him. She had to find out. Fear had her scurrying to find her mother and let her know of her plans. "I have to check," she said with tears in her eyes.

"You should let Elijah or Isaac take you."

"I don't want to ruin their plans."

"Charlie…"

"I'll be fine. The roads are fine."

"At least ask Isaac if you can use his sleigh."

She agreed and ran to see if he minded. When he argued about taking her, she didn't relent and finally her cousin gave in.

Her mother nodded. "Take your time. If Charlotte is in labor, they may need you to watch the little ones, but first you have to get there safely." She paused. "You need to see Nathaniel," she said astutely. "You care a great deal for him."

Charlie blushed. "Is it that obvious?"

"Only to your mother," *Mam* said. "And I know he cares for you, too."

"You think so?" she whispered, pleased, hoping that it was really true and she hadn't imagined the feelings between them.

"I do. Call it a mother's gift." She urged her toward the door. "Travel safely, *dochter*. If you need me for anything, send word and I'll come."

Charlie raced to Isaac's sleigh and headed toward the Abram Peachy residence. She'd driven her cousins' sleighs before, so she felt confident as she drove. When she arrived at the Abram Peachy farm, she saw two buggies parked side by side in the barnyard. She frowned as she parked the sleigh alongside the buggies and tied up the horses. She then climbed the porch steps and knocked. The door opened within seconds. "Jacob," she greeted. "Is everything *oll recht*? When you didn't come, I became worried."

"*Mam's* having the baby." He looked solemn as he stepped back and gestured her inside.

"How is she?"

"I don't know. Something's wrong, I think. Nate left to get the midwife."

"Is she in her room?"

He nodded.

"May I go up and see her? Maybe I can help."

He looked relieved. "*Ja*, if she'll let you. *Dat's* in the kitchen. She didn't want him in the room. I think 'tis because he becomes upset to see her in pain. Mary Elizabeth left earlier to spend the afternoon with Mark's family. Ruth and Harley went with her. Mae Ann left with Nate."

Charlie was trembling as she went up to the second floor and approached the couple's bedroom. She heard the woman cry out and rushed to help. She stood at the closed door a second before another cry prompted her to open it. "Charlotte?" she called out. "'Tis Charlie. May I come in?" There was another sharp cry then silence. She couldn't see around an interior wall to the bed. *"Charlotte?"*

When the woman didn't answer, Charlie went in. Nate's *mam* was on the bed, propped up on pillows. She looked pale and her eyes were closed.

Charlie approached slowly. "Hey, *Mam*," she said softly. "How can I help?"

Her eyes flickered open, and the woman offered her a weak smile. "Charlie."

"*Ja*, 'tis me." Encouraged, she approached. "I understand that Nate went for the midwife. I'd like to stay until she comes if you'll let me."

"*Ja*, please stay." She laid her hands on her abdomen as she shifted in the bed. "I'm afraid," Charlotte admitted. "The baby isn't due yet."

Charlie reached for her hand. "Two weeks either way is normal. This isn't your first baby. I'm sure he or she will be fine."

Charlotte grimaced as a contraction tightened her belly.

"Blow through your mouth," Charlie reminded her. "Little puffs. I'm sure you did that with Mae Ann and Harley, *ja*?"

Obeying immediately, Nate's mother blew in and out in short breaths. Charlie recognized when the pain left her as she quieted and briefly closed her eyes.

"Is the midwife here yet?" she asked weakly.

"*Nay*, not yet, but I'm sure she will be soon."

The woman relaxed as her pain eased. "I understand that you like being *schuul-*teacher," she said.

"*Ja*, I do. I love working with children."

"I miss seeing you every day."

"I miss you," Charlie said.

"You're perfect for the job—until you marry and have children of your own."

Charlie's heart gave a lurch. "I would like children someday," she murmured. Had Nate informed his parents that they were seeing each other? She studied his stepmother and saw nothing in her expression that suggested the woman knew. She sighed as she realized that Nate wasn't ready for others to know.

"Nate thinks you're a wonderful teacher," Charlotte said.

Charlie blinked. "He does?"

"*Ja*. Do you know he spoke with the bishop about you?"

She stiffened, grew chilled. "He talked to the bishop?"

The woman shook her head. "I don't know what he said but it wasn't long afterward that you were offered the position."

"And you think Nate had something to do with it?"

His mother grimaced. Her body tightened

with another contraction and she managed to gasp, "*Nay.* You got that on your own." She panted as previously instructed to get through the pain. Suddenly, she cried out. "Charlie, I can feel the baby coming!"

Charlie pushed aside her own upset as she looked for something to wrap the infant in. There was a small quilt on the dresser, and she reached for it. She held up the quilt. "I'm sorry, 'tis a beautiful blanket but we need it." She'd never delivered a baby before. But she could do it, she thought. She would deliver this baby, because she was the only one here and God must have wanted her to help. "Do you feel like pushing?" she asked, her heart racing wildly.

"*Ja!*" she cried out as Charlie laid the quilt across the bed in the best position to set the baby down after he was born.

A short time later a tiny angry cry filled the room as a new Peachy son was born. Charlie carefully lay the child on the quilt. The door burst open and the midwife entered, followed closely by Nate.

Nate took one look at her with the baby and his eyes widened.

"You should leave," the midwife said to Nate. "I'll call you when they're ready." The woman had come forward to inspect mother and baby.

After briefly meeting Nate's gaze, Charlie looked away. She felt betrayed. He hadn't told her the truth when he'd said he believed in her. It had been a lie. He hadn't trusted that she'd get the teaching job on her own and so he'd talked with the elders even though she'd asked him not to. Even after she'd explained why. A lump rose to her throat as she stood back and watched the midwife examine her patients.

"Are they well?" she asked anxiously.

The midwife, a woman by the name of Sarah Locke, smiled. "They're fine." She eyed Charlie intently. "You delivered her baby," she said.

Charlie nodded. "I had to use the quilt." She glanced toward the baby's mother, who now lovingly cradled her infant son. "I'm sorry."

Charlotte frowned. "Why?"

"I ruined it. I'll make you another quilt. Until then, I'll go to Leah's store and buy you a new one."

The new mother laughed. "I don't need another quilt, Charlie. You did *gut*. Stop second-guessing yourself." Her expression grew serious. "*Danki* for being there for me."

She nodded. "I'm glad I could help."

"Would you tell Abram to come up?"

"I'll head down now." Charlie stepped closer for another look at the baby. "Congratulations on your son."

"*Danki.*" Charlotte Peachy was beaming. She looked pale and exhausted but gloriously happy.

She went downstairs to tell everyone the news. "Sarah said that you can go up now," she said as she grabbed her coat and put it on. She felt the intensity of Nate's gaze but wouldn't look at him. "I have to go."

He touched her arm. "Charlie."

"I have to go," she repeated in a strangled voice. The others had left the room and she could hear them climbing the steps to see the new addition to their family.

"Charlie, what's wrong?" He looked concerned and dumbfounded at her behavior.

"You didn't trust me," she whispered achingly. "You didn't listen and you didn't trust me."

Then she raced out the door to her sleigh and drove home. She understood now that he didn't love her the way she'd hoped. Her tears fell as she steered the sleigh over the snow-packed street. She brushed them away as she continued to cry. When she got home, she went up to her room. Someone knocked seconds later. When she didn't answer, the door opened and Ellie entered.

"Charlie, what happened? What's wrong? Did something happen to Charlotte?" She frowned as she sat on the side of Charlie's bed. "You've been crying."

"I'm fine." She forced a smile. "Charlotte just gave birth to a healthy son."

Ellie beamed. "That's wonderful."

"I delivered him."

Her sister's mouth dropped open. "*You* did?"

Tears filled her eyes as she nodded. "You don't believe I'm capable of it, do you?"

"*Nay*, 'tis not that!" Ellie reached out to rub Charlie's arm. "I just thought that a midwife would be there…or another woman in the *haus*."

"Nate left to get her, but the baby couldn't wait any longer."

"And you were there for her." Ellie grinned. "You are something, aren't you?"

She drew a sharp breath. "Am I?"

"I'm sure Nate was impressed." Her sister paused. "You love him." She lowered her brow. "*Ach nay*, something went wrong between the two of you."

Charlie shot her a look. "I—how did you know?"

"You're my sister. I know you. I've seen the way the two of you look when you're together. It was easy to see how you feel about him." She smiled. "And how he feels about you."

She rubbed a hand across her aching forehead. "Doesn't matter."

Ellie's brow furrowed. "What do you mean?"

"It means that Nate doesn't feel the same way about me as I do about him." The pain in her chest grew. "He doesn't trust that I can do anything successfully on my own."

"I doubt he feels that way now. Not after delivering his brother."

Charlie snorted. "Too late—and 'tis not the same. Do you know what I learned? Nate spoke to Bishop John about me…to help me get the teaching position."

"So? What is wrong with that?"

"After I specifically asked him not to!" she cried as she sat up. "I wanted to get the job on my own, Ellie. I know I've made mistakes in the past, but I needed to know that the elders considered me the best person for the job. Apparently, they needed Nate to convince them of it."

With a murmur of sympathy, Ellie tugged her into her arms. "I don't believe that's how Nate feels. Honestly? I believe he loves you so much he couldn't help but interfere. He wants you to be happy."

"Then he should have listened to me."

"*Ja*, perhaps," Ellie said, surprising her. "But he is a man and he's in love, and men in love sometimes do dumb things."

"He believes I need a keeper."

Her sister's expression softened. "Perhaps you do. And Nate is perfect for you." Ellie smirked. "Did you need me to recommend him?"

"*Nay.*" Charlie experienced a lessening of her hurt and anger. She bit her lip. "How can I get past the fact that he lied to me? And he never actually said that he loves me."

"I think you're mistaken. I don't believe for a minute that Nate would lie to you. About your love for him—have you told him how you feel?"

She frowned. "*Nay*, how could I when I don't know if he really loves me? He said he wants to court me, but I don't know…"

To Charlie's shock, Ellie laughed. "*Ja*," she said, still chuckling, "the both of you are most definitely in love."

"Too late. I wasn't nice to him when I left."

"It will all work out in the end."

Regretting her behavior, Charlie closed her eyes. "I hope so." She offered a silent prayer that it would be so.

Chapter Sixteen

Nate stood in the corner of his parents' room and looked on as his father held his newborn son. *Dat* was seated on the edge of his wife's bed. His stepmother lay, resting, propped up by several pillows. There was tenderness in her expression and a smile of happiness on her lips as she watched her husband with their baby. His siblings were behind their father. Each one exclaimed over the perfection of the tiny life. Harley, the baby until Lucas was born, studied his brother with fascination. Ruth and Mae begged to hold Lucas and were told they'd each have a chance to hold him later.

As he quietly listened to everyone in the room, he found his thoughts going to Charlie and the abrupt way she'd left. She'd looked angry and hurt. What could he have done to upset her?

Charlie had delivered his baby brother! The fact still gave him pause. After his initial shock, he should have known not to be surprised. She was a capable, amazing young woman with spirit and gumption, which he loved and appreciated about her. Charlie Stoltzfus could do anything she set her mind to, he realized. Hadn't she broken clear through his resistance to win his heart?

He loved her and wanted her as his wife with every breath he took. She'd literally changed his life for the better. In truth, he wished he could forget the courting stage and wed her tomorrow.

Everyone in the room exclaimed over the new baby. Nate managed a smile as he saw Mae Ann and then his little brother Harley lean in to give his new baby brother a soft kiss on his tiny forehead. At their father's suggestion, everyone left the room so that mother and son could sleep. Nate, the last to leave, turned to go.

"Nathaniel," his mother called. He halted and faced her. "Where's Charlie? I expected her to see me before she left."

"She seemed upset and in a hurry to leave,"

he said with concern. "She wouldn't talk or look at me when she came downstairs."

His *mam* frowned. "That's not right," she murmured. "The girl cares for you."

Nate shook his head. "I don't know if she does."

"She loves you. Of that, I have no doubt. Why do you think she came racing over here when we didn't show up for Second Christmas dinner? She was afraid something happened to you. She was worried."

"I…"

"You love her. I know you do. So why are you still home? Why haven't you gone after her?"

"You just had a baby," he began.

"And you want a life. Do you think I haven't noticed how you longed to spend time with her?"

"Maybe she changed her mind and decided I'm too old for her."

Mam laughed. "Absolutely not. That's not who Charlie is. Do you know that she used to avoid coming here when she knew you'd be around?" She smiled. "She was nervous around you because she cared for you even then."

He arched an eyebrow. "The Charlie I know isn't afraid of anything."

She regarded him with a soft expression.

"*Ja*, she is. You were so far out of her reach she thought she'd never have you."

"She needs a keeper."

His mother laughed. "*Ja*, she does."

"I'm not a *gut* one," he said with a frown. "Did *Dat* tell you about Emma?"

Her face softened. "*Ja*, he did. And we both feel the same. You did nothing wrong. Her death wasn't your fault. You were a boy and you tried everything you could to help her. God doesn't help those who don't help themselves. You didn't fail Emma and you won't fail Charlie."

Was it true? In his youth, had he wrongfully taken the blame for something he'd had no control over? "I love Charlie. I don't want her to change. I just want to be there for her every day in case she needs me." He paused. "For the rest of our lives."

"Then go!" She gestured toward the door. "I've always loved Charlie. I wouldn't mind having her as my *soohn*'s wife." She lay back against the pillows and closed her eyes. "Now go tell that woman of yours how much you love her."

Nate smiled. "*Ja, Mam.*"

Charlie lay in bed, fighting tears. The ache in her heart wouldn't go away. She loved

Nate, but how could they have a life together if he didn't respect or trust her?

Her sister had left the room. It was later in the day, and Ellie must have made excuses for her and explained about the baby delivery, because no one had come upstairs to bother her. And for that she was thankful.

She still loved Nate and she always would. Why hadn't he listened? Why couldn't he have trusted her to become a teacher on her own? When he'd offered to talk with his father, the deacon, she'd said no. She didn't want him to interfere. But that he had anyway hurt beyond measure.

"Charlie!"

Charlie rose at her mother's call. *"Ja, Mam?"*

"You have a visitor!"

"Who is it?"

"Why don't you come down and see."

Heart racing as she thought of Nate, she got up off the bed and descended the stairs. To her shock, her visitor was Abram Peachy, Nate's father.

"Abram," she gasped. "I didn't expect to see you. Is Charlotte and your baby *oll recht*?"

"They are fine. We've chosen a name for him—Lucas."

"Lucas." She smiled. "I like it." She eyed

him curiously. "If everyone's fine, then why have you come?"

"To thank you for what you did today. I don't know how my wife would have done it without you. You have been a blessing to our family, Charlie, and for a long time. 'Tis why I told the elders you'd be a *gut* teacher and they agreed."

Charlie gazed at him speechless. "*You* recommended me for the job?"

"*Ja.*" He eyed her with concern. "You seem surprised."

"I thought I got the job because of Nate. I found out that he spoke with Bishop John."

Abram looked surprised. "He did?"

"*Ja.* Charlotte told me."

His brow cleared. "Ah! That must have been after we'd already made our choice." He smiled. "We made the decision to offer you the job before we left for Indiana."

"Then I got the position on my own?"

"*Ja*, of course. Why would you think otherwise?"

She shrugged. "No reason." She grinned, happy that she'd been offered the teacher job based on her own merits. But that didn't excuse the fact that Nate thought she couldn't have.

"I should get home."

Charlie nodded. Everyone would be gathering at Amos King's for church on Sunday. "I'll see you at Amos and Mae's." She followed him to the door. Nate was coming up the steps as his father was leaving.

"Dat," he said with surprise.

"Nate. Come to see Charlie, have you?" he said with a twinkle.

"If she will talk with me." His eyes shifted to lock gazes with her. "Charlie."

"I'll see you at home, *soohn*," Abram said before he left.

She started to turn away as Nate rushed up the steps and into the house. He gently caught her arm. "Charlie."

She scowled at him. "What are you doing here, Nathaniel Peachy?"

He seemed taken aback by her hostility. And despite her anger with him, she loved him and hated to see his pain. "What do you want?" she asked with a sigh.

"I need to talk with you."

"I *don't* need to talk with you." She gave him her back.

"Charlie, I love you."

She stiffened, unwilling to believe she'd heard correctly. He touched her shoulder before his hand slid up to cup her nape. "Nathaniel."

"I mean it, Charlie. I thought to be patient

and take things slowly, but I can't do it anymore. I had to tell you today. I love you and I want us to be together forever." She saw him swallow hard. "I want to marry you."

Charlie closed her eyes on a wave of pain. "You don't think I can do things on my own." His caressing fingers on her neck stilled.

"*Ja*, I do. I believe in you. I told you that."

"*Ja*, words were all they were, but I know the truth." She faced him defiantly. "You went to Bishop John. You talked about me! You didn't think I could win the teaching position on my own."

"*Ja*, I did. And, *ja*, I admit talking with him. You amaze me, Charlie. I went to see John so that I could tell him about everything you did for me and Jacob. I couldn't not tell him. I love you and I needed to tell someone how wonderful you are, and I couldn't talk about you with anyone else!"

She gazed at him with mouth agape. "You think I'm wonderful?"

His expression softened. "You are wonderful, Charlie. And amazing, and I want you for my wife."

"You want to be my keeper," she said as the pain and anger she'd been feeling began to subside.

"I want to be your definition of a keeper.

I want to be your husband, the one who will love you until death parts us…the woman I want to have children with." He stopped and his face filled with worry. "That is if you still want children after what you did today."

"And what did I do?" she teased softly. She really did love this misguided man, and she would continue to love him for a lifetime.

"Deliver a baby—my *bruder*. You saw what mothers must endure to have children."

Charlie laughed. When he looked stung, she softened her laughter to an affectionate smile. "I know what women go through while giving birth. How can I not? Do you think I've never seen birthing before? I have. But I must confess that I haven't been the only one in the room before today. 'Tis worth it, you know…the pain of childbirth, for once you hold a baby in your arms, you understand. All good things come to those who understand. And, Nate? I understand that I'd like nothing more than to be your wife and give you children."

Nate gazed at her with rapture. "You're certain? That I'm the right man?"

"I'm absolutely, positively certain." She reached for his hand. "And Nathaniel? I don't want to hear any more about the difference in our ages. Age means nothing when there is love." She gave him a tender smile. "And I love you with all my heart." She blinked at him as her eyes suddenly filled with tears. "I thought you didn't believe in me."

"I did. I do." He reached out to run his hand up her arm. "I believe in you and I don't want you to change."

"Not even a little bit?" she joked.

He tugged her closer until she could feel the warmth in his gaze within the beat of her heart. "Not even a little bit."

"I think you might regret saying that."

Nate laughed. "Maybe." He took both of her hands.

Charlie's mother came out of a room and headed toward the stairs. She froze when she saw them. "Nate!"

"*Hallo*, Missy. I've come to talk with Charlie." He beamed down at the woman whose hands he held.

She smiled. "I see. And how is your new baby *bruder*?"

"Lucas is fine. He's healthy and *Mam* and *Dat* are extremely happy and pleased that Charlie was there to help him into the world."

"Will you be going to the Amos Kings' for church service?" her mother asked him.

"I'll be there."

"*Gut*." She continued past them to ascend

the stairs, pausing once on the steps to smile down at them. "'Tis *gut* to see you here, Nathaniel." Then she disappeared from sight as she reached the second floor.

"I think my *mudder* knows how we feel about each other."

"*Ja*, I think so, too," he said, raising their held hands. "She doesn't seem to mind." He hugged her briefly then released her. "I should go, but I'll see you tomorrow."

She smiled as she bobbed her head. "Be careful going home," she said softly.

She followed him outside onto the porch. The air was brisk and Nate looked back, frowned and said, "Get back inside before you catch your death."

"*Ja*, Nathaniel."

Charlie watched the man she loved drive away. She looked forward to spending the future with him. His behavior in front of her mother made it clear that he was ready to announce their relationship to everyone. *He loves me.*

She sent up a silent prayer of thanks to the Lord for granting her heart's desire.

Two days after Second Christmas brought snow flurries that fluttered down to earth in glorious white wonder. As she stood at the window at home, she wondered when Nate would arrive. Because his family hadn't enjoyed the holiday due to the baby's birth, they were to celebrate it today.

She hadn't seen him yesterday. The short separation after his declaration of love seemed like forever. She missed him. Where was he? She'd expected him here by now.

Hugging herself, Charlie gazed out into the barnyard. Suddenly, she was surrounded by masculine arms and pulled back to rest against someone's chest. "You had better be Nathaniel Peachy or I won't be responsible for my actions."

He laughed, and the sound was so lighthearted and joyful that she tugged out of his arms to face him. "Merry do-over Christmas, Charlie."

She enjoyed looking at him. His blue eyes sparkled. He looked relaxed…and happy and more than content. "I thought you'd never get here," she breathed.

"I've been here awhile," he admitted.

She froze. "You have?" Why hadn't he come to see her sooner?

"I stopped to talk with the bishop."

Charlie scowled. "What for?"

"To ask permission to marry you."

"You did?" she whispered with wonder.

A smile continued to hover on his lips. There was tenderness in his expression and warmth and love in his blue gaze. "*Ja*, and the deacon…and then I cornered your father to ask for his blessing."

"You did?"

He chuckled as he reached out to tuck in a lock of stray hair. "I did."

"And did you get my *vadder*'s blessing?"

"*Ja.*" He leaned in until they touched foreheads. "'Tis official. Everyone approves and so now you will have to marry me." His smile dimmed a little as he straightened. "We'll have to wait a year until the month of weddings. I know it will be the longest year of my life, but at least I'm allowed to court you openly."

"So in a year, I'll become your keeper. And you'll be mine," she said breathlessly. "My husband."

"I'll be forever yours." He handed her a wrapped package. "Merry Christmas, love. I'm sorry I couldn't give you this sooner." A smile hovered about his lips. "Open it."

With hands that shook, she unwrapped the package and gasped. "'Tis a wooden mare and her colt!"

He nodded. "*Ja*, do you like them?"

"I love them!" She reached out to touch his

face. "They are as beautiful as the other horse you made me." She played with the ends of his hair. "How do you know me so well?"

He shrugged. She reached toward a table where she'd set Nate's gift earlier. "Merry Christmas," she whispered as she handed him a box. "'Tis not as nice as the one you gave me." Inside she'd placed the new scarf she'd bought for him and something she'd made for him on her own. Something silly that she hoped he'd nevertheless appreciate.

The wrapping came off, and Nate opened the cardboard flaps. He saw the scarf first and grinned at her.

"For when you are cold," she said. "I'm sorry I didn't make it for you. I haven't mastered the art of knitting yet, but I will." She watched as he lifted the scarf out of the box and put it around his neck. He looked at what was left inside the box and started to laugh. "Ingredients for peanut butter and jam sandwiches," he said with a twinkle of delight in his blue eyes.

"I made all three—the jam, the peanut butter and the bread."

He looked at her with such love in his eyes that she caught her breath. "You will make me the best wife and keeper."

"Do you think so?" She felt a warmth that brought tears of happiness to her eyes.

"*Ja*, I do." His expression darkened for a moment, and Charlie suffered a moment of fear. "There is something I have to tell you. If you change your mind about me, I'll understand."

She swallowed hard. "What is it?"

"Do you want to know why I've kept my distance from you? Why I'm insistent about keeping you safe?"

She nodded, but felt unsure.

He reached for her hands and held them. "I had a sweetheart when I was sixteen. Her name was Emma," he began. "She was a bit reckless and impulsive. She always seemed to crave excitement. I cared for her a great deal, and I thought she cared for me. Maybe she did and maybe she didn't. Either way, she didn't listen to me when I warned her against her English friends. One night she had slipped out of her house to go joyriding with them. The car crashed and the four *Englishers* were seriously hurt. Emma was killed instantly."

"Nate," she breathed, watching him, her heart filled with compassion for a wounded young man who'd lost someone he'd loved.

He released one of her hands to caress her face. "The way I felt for her is nothing like

I feel for you, Charlie. I was a boy. I didn't know what love was until my love for you."

She blinked rapidly. She tugged her hand free, lay her head on his chest and slipped her arms about him in a heartfelt hug.

"Charlie," he said and she pulled back. "That's not all."

Alarmed, she could only gaze at him. "I've had a hard time with Emma's death because I saw it happen. The accident. I was the first on the scene and knew immediately that she was dead."

"Oh, Nate…" She raised up on her toes to kiss his cheek, his chin, until she finally settled a sweet kiss against his mouth. "I'm sorry."

He blinked. "I felt I'd failed her, Charlie. For a long time, I was afraid I'd fail you, too."

"And now?" She waited with bated breath.

"I'm older and wiser. I realize that I'm not the same person I was back then, and you're most definitely not Emma. You're Charlie, the woman I love. The only woman I've ever truly loved."

Epilogue

❧

Christmas Day, Two Years Later

A baby's cry had Nate running up the steps
to the master bedroom in their farmhouse. He
halted on the threshold and caught his breath.
His wife lay in bed, cradling their new baby.
She looked radiant as she smiled at the infant
in her arms. He'd been waiting downstairs it
seemed like forever. If he'd had his way, he
would have stayed right beside her, but the
midwife had insisted that no men were allowed in the room during the childbirth.

Charlie glanced over to see him in the
doorway. "Nathaniel," she said as she reached
out a hand toward him. "Come and meet your
son."

With a rush of love, he hurried to her side.
He swallowed against a suddenly tight throat.

He didn't fight the tears that sprang to his eyes and trailed down his cheeks. "A son," he whispered.

"Congratulations, Nate." Missy Stoltzfus stood on the other side of the room, watching with a warm smile.

He beamed at her through his tears before turning back to his wife, the woman he adored above all others. He sensed that his mother-in-law and the midwife had left the room to give them privacy. "I love you, *Mam*," he said, referring to her new status.

She jerked with surprise, then her features softened with a bright smile. "I guess I'll have to get used to him calling me that." She beamed down at her son. "'Tis a special gift, becoming a mother."

"You're my special gift. My Christmas gift for always," he murmured since it was during the Christmas season two years ago that he'd won approval from the church elders and their parents to take Charlie to wife. No one seemed bothered by the fact that he was older than she was by seven years. And he wondered now why he'd allowed it to bother him in the first place. He reached out to stroke his infant son's cheek. "Merry Christmas, *soohn*."

"Our Christmas blessing," Charlie said

with happiness and love for him and their newborn in her expression.

"What will we name him?"

"I was thinking of Zacharias."

"Or Zachary," he murmured, liking both.

"Or Ezekiel," she said. "We could call him Zeke."

"*Ja*. I like that name best." He bent and brushed a kiss against her forehead. "You don't regret giving up your teaching job?"

She shook her head. "How can I? I have you and now, as if God has decided that we don't have enough happiness, a child of our own. Nothing can compare to the life you've given me."

"Amen," he breathed as he leaned in to kiss her. "Merry Christmas, my love."

"Merry Christmas, husband," she said with tears glistening in her beautiful green eyes, eyes he would forever be lost in—and love.

* * * * *

If you loved this story,
check out the other books
in Rebecca Kertz's miniseries
Women of Lancaster County:

A Secret Amish Love
Her Amish Christmas Sweetheart
Her Forgiving Amish Heart

Available now from Love Inspired!

Find more great reads at
www.LoveInspired.com

Dear Reader,

Welcome back to Happiness, Pennsylvania. In my Women of Lancaster County series, we've met three Stoltzfus sisters so far: Nell, Meg and Leah. *Her Amish Christmas Gift* tells the story of Charlie Stoltzfus, the youngest of the five sisters, and the man she longs for, Nathaniel Peachy. Charlie was considered a wild child during her youth but she's older and wiser now. Unfortunately, Nate considers her nothing more than an impulsive young girl whose actions often get her into trouble. While he thinks about the possibility of finding her a suitable husband, he never follows through, because the thought of Charlie with another man greatly disturbs him. And when his brother's accident suddenly brings them into close contact while his brother heals, Nate finds himself looking forward to seeing Charlie each day. But as his feelings for her grow, so does the realization that he isn't the right man for her. Or is he?

I hope you enjoy Charlie and Nate's story as much as I did writing it. If you haven't read the books about Charlie's sisters, you may want to pick up copies of *Her Secret Amish Love* (Nell), *Her Amish Christmas*

Sweetheart (Meg) and *Her Forgiving Amish Heart* (Leah). Each sister struggles to find her own special love. Sometimes the road to happiness is a bumpy one, but the journey of love's discovery is well worth it in the end.

Blessings and love,

Rebecca Kertz

Get 4 FREE REWARDS!

We'll send you 2 FREE Books plus 2 FREE Mystery Gifts.

Love Inspired® Suspense books feature Christian characters facing challenges to their faith... and lives.

FREE
Value Over
$20

YES! Please send me 2 FREE Love Inspired® Suspense novels and my 2 FREE mystery gifts (gifts are worth about $10 retail). After receiving them, if I don't wish to receive any more books, I can return the shipping statement marked "cancel." If I don't cancel, I will receive 4 brand-new novels every month and be billed just $5.24 each for the regular-print edition or $5.74 each for the larger-print edition in the U.S., or $5.74 each for the regular-print edition or $6.24 each for the larger-print edition in Canada. That's a savings of at least 13% off the cover price. It's quite a bargain! Shipping and handling is just 50¢ per book in the U.S. and 75¢ per book in Canada.* I understand that accepting the 2 free books and gifts places me under no obligation to buy anything. I can always return a shipment and cancel at any time. The free books and gifts are mine to keep no matter what I decide.

Choose one: ☐ **Love Inspired® Suspense Regular-Print** (153/353 IDN GMY5)   ☐ **Love Inspired® Suspense Larger-Print** (107/307 IDN GMY5)

Name (please print)

Address   Apt. #

City   State/Province   Zip/Postal Code

Mail to the Reader Service:
IN U.S.A.: P.O. Box 1341, Buffalo, NY 14240-8531
IN CANADA: P.O. Box 603, Fort Erie, Ontario L2A 5X3

Want to try 2 free books from another series! Call 1-800-873-8635 or visit www.ReaderService.com.

---

*Terms and prices subject to change without notice. Prices do not include applicable taxes. Sales tax applicable in N.Y. Canadian residents will be charged applicable taxes. Offer not valid in Quebec. This offer is limited to one order per household. Books received may not be as shown. Not valid for current subscribers to Love Inspired Suspense books. All orders subject to approval. Credit or debit balances in a customer's account(s) may be offset by any other outstanding balance owed by or to the customer. Please allow 4 to 6 weeks for delivery. Offer available while quantities last.

Your Privacy—The Reader Service is committed to protecting your privacy. Our Privacy Policy is available online at www.ReaderService.com or upon request from the Reader Service. We make a portion of our mailing list available to reputable third parties that offer products we believe may interest you. If you prefer that we not exchange your name with third parties, or if you wish to clarify or modify your communication preferences, please visit us at www.ReaderService.com/consumerschoice or write to us at Reader Service Preference Service, P.O. Box 9062, Buffalo, NY 14240-9062. Include your complete name and address.

LIS19

Get 4 FREE REWARDS!

We'll send you 2 FREE Books plus 2 FREE Mystery Gifts.

Harlequin® Heartwarming™ Larger-Print books feature traditional values of home, family, community and—most of all—love.

FREE Value Over $20

YES! Please send me 2 FREE Harlequin® Heartwarming™ Larger-Print novels and my 2 FREE mystery gifts (gifts worth about $10 retail). After receiving them, if I don't wish to receive any more books, I can return the shipping statement marked "cancel." If I don't cancel, I will receive 4 brand-new larger-print novels every month and be billed just $5.49 per book in the U.S. or $6.24 per book in Canada. That's a savings of at least 19% off the cover price. It's quite a bargain! Shipping and handling is just 50¢ per book in the U.S. and 75¢ per book in Canada.* I understand that accepting the 2 free books and gifts places me under no obligation to buy anything. I can always return a shipment and cancel at any time. The free books and gifts are mine to keep no matter what I decide.

161/361 IDN GMY3

Name (please print)

Address   Apt. #

City   State/Province   Zip/Postal Code

Mail to the Reader Service:
IN U.S.A.: P.O. Box 1341, Buffalo, NY 14240-8531
IN CANADA: P.O. Box 603, Fort Erie, Ontario L2A 5X3

Want to try 2 free books from another series? Call 1-800-873-8635 or visit www.ReaderService.com.

---

*Terms and prices subject to change without notice. Prices do not include applicable taxes. Sales tax applicable in N.Y. Canadian residents will be charged applicable taxes. Offer not valid in Quebec. This offer is limited to one order per household. Books received may not be as shown. Not valid for current subscribers to Harlequin Heartwarming Larger-Print books. All orders subject to approval. Credit or debit balances in a customer's account(s) may be offset by any other outstanding balance owed by or to the customer. Please allow 4 to 6 weeks for delivery. Offer available while quantities last.

Your Privacy—The Reader Service is committed to protecting your privacy. Our Privacy Policy is available online at www.ReaderService.com or upon request from the Reader Service. We make a portion of our mailing list available to reputable third parties that offer products we believe may interest you. If you prefer that we not exchange your name with third parties, or if you wish to clarify or modify your communication preferences, please visit us at www.ReaderService.com/consumerschoice or write to us at Reader Service Preference Service, P.O. Box 9062, Buffalo, NY 14240-9062. Include your complete name and address.

HW19

HOME on the RANCH

HRCBPA18R